Death's Head

Death's Head

Jonathan Ross

St. Martin's Press
New York

Library of Congress Cataloging in Publication Data

Ross, Jonathan, 1916-
   Death's head.

   I. Title.
PR6068.0835D4   1983   823'.914   83-2932
ISBN 0-312-18882-X

First published in Great Britain by Constable and Company Ltd.

First U.S. Edition
10 9 8 7 6 5 4 3 2 1

Death's Head

I

For a Station Sergeant, ten minutes past five in the morning in a comatose town is a time for clearing the accumulated paperwork and looking forward to six o'clock and going home to a bed already warmed by a sleeping wife.

It had been a busy night for Sergeant Llewellyn, an unceasing happening of domestic disturbances, burglaries and shop-breakings, drunken brawls and traffic accidents. Nobody had been murdered, for which he was profoundly grateful. But he had been burdened with a newly-promoted Duty Inspector, now out checking the beats with a fledgeling inspector's unwanted zeal, capable of returning to the station coincidentally with the sergeant's need for a forbidden cigarette.

Busy at his desk, he felt a brief niggle of irritation towards the old man entering through the swing doors, bringing in with him from outside the dawn chorus of birds. He was skeletally emaciated, cadaverous and beak-nosed with an Elizabethan beard and moustache, his white hair bushing out from beneath a homburg hat moss-green from exposure to years of weather. Behind spectacles, one lens of which was cracked with a fragment missing, his eyes were faded and watery blue. Indifferent to the balminess of a dying August night, he wore a heavy Inverness-caped overcoat and carried a rolled-up blanket and a walking stick. From a distance, or in a poor light, he would look professorially distinguished; close to, he was unmistakably shabby and malodorously uncaring of his personal hygiene.

The sergeant knew him well. He was Dominic Charles Lockersbie of No Fixed Abode, the wreckage of a former schoolteacher, a man who had lost his wife and with her his will to live; anaesthetizing his bereavement with alcohol to an

5

extent by which he also lost by early retirement his assistant mastership at a minor public school and the staff house that went with it. He carried his drunkenness with dignity and was able, by virtue of his small pension, to suffer few periods of soberness in which to remember.

He was always a scrupulously courteous and gentle man, and the police showed him a grossly improper partiality in refusing ever to assess the state of his drunkenness as being unlawful and requiring arrest. At night, should his brain and legs co-ordinate sufficiently for walking, he made his way to the graveyard in which his wife was buried and slept in the porch of the church of Saint Boniface. There, cocooned in his blanket, he became unofficially an invisible non-person to any patrolling constable stepping over him to check the security of the church.

Standing at the Enquiry Office counter, he laid his stick on it and lifted his hat. 'Good morning, Sergeant Llewellyn,' he said. His voice was reedy, his words carefully articulated.

'Morning, Mr Lockersbie.' Never a man to be addressed by his first name, he was, the sergeant estimated, about 75 per cent drunk, the fruity aroma of wine following his words. 'You're about early.'

'I haven't been to bed at all. Which is why . . .' He lost the thread of what he had been about to say, his eyes wobbling to look over the sergeant's head. 'I feel obliged to inform you that I have seen a dead man.'

'I see.' Llewellyn said it gravely and with an assumed understanding. 'Where was this?' A few weeks earlier it had been a spectral black dog following at his heels and he had brought its unseen presence into the station with him, being jocularly advised to get a collar and lead and a licence for it. Lockersbie's hallucinations had in them none of the alcoholic's commonplace variegated snakes or swarms of gigantic spiders, none of the whispering, threatening voices coming from the high corners of a room.

'Pardon me, dear boy.' Turning his back on him, he fumbled beneath his cape and drank from a bottle. Facing him again, he

6

said, 'A necessity, not an indulgence. Shock, you know.' He put the bottle away. It had obviously fuelled his usual garrulity. 'At the church, in my doorway. It was horrible, quite horrible. When I saw him I was angry. I thought, unjustly as it turned out, that he was one of those disgusting methylated spirits drinkers trespassing on my little residence. And probably verminous too. But I was mistaken.'

'You say he was dead?'

'Quite definitely.'

'How do you know he was?' The sergeant was making notes, although he believed it to be wasted effort.

'I really do recognize death when I see it, having had a passing acquaintance with it.' He had, too, with a Military Cross to prove it.

'Wouldn't it be dark?'

'Moonlight, dear boy. I quote: *The moon doth with delight, Look round her when the heavens are bare.* Wordsworth,' he said. 'You are familiar with him?'

'Not that much, but I've heard him mentioned. Why did you think he was dead?'

'He was ghastly pale and quite unmoving. I touched him on the shoulder – he was sitting, leaning against the door – and said, "Pardon my disturbing you, sir, but you are occupying my bed." He never moved. He never answered me at all. Which was when I realized that I had been addressing a dead man.'

'What did you do then?'

'I fled, dear boy, in mortal terror, having no wish to share my doorway with the dead.'

'Did he have any injuries?' Llewellyn asked patiently. 'Bullet wounds? Lacerations? Had he been bleeding?'

Lockersbie frowned thoughtfully. 'I saw none of those, dear boy. Possibly he died from natural causes.'

'And you would be able to recognize that from, say, unconsciousness? In the dark?' He wanted also to say 'And in your condition?' but held it back.

'Dear me, yes. Quite unmistakably so.'

'You're sure it wasn't another dr . . .' He cut his question short, needing to be tactful and having no wish to hurt the old man's feelings. 'Sorry, I meant another homeless man sleeping it off?'

Lockersbie gazed at him; mildly, but also as though he were a fourth-former having the cheek to question his parsing of a sentence. 'He was dead, dear boy. You may accept my assurance of that. Shouldn't you be sending somebody there?'

'When I've all the details, Mr Lockersbie. If he's dead he won't be wandering off. If he isn't, we don't have a problem.' The sergeant took his defeat impassively. 'Can you describe him? His clothing for a start?'

Lockersbie shook his head. 'Regrettably not. He was mostly in the shadows. But I think a dark suit. No hat, of course. People don't wear them now, do they?'

'A young man? Middle-aged? Elderly?'

'He appeared as though he had endured life long enough. I believe you would call him middle-aged. An intelligent face, I should say, although his mouth was open. Not,' he said calmly, 'the sort of man I would expect to be reduced to sharing my bed.'

'Clean-shaven?'

'He had neither beard nor moustache.'

None of this sounded hallucinatory and Llewellyn was uncomfortably aware that he should take him seriously. 'His hair, Mr Lockersbie. Dark, fair or in between?'

He frowned again. 'Moonlight is deceptive, dear boy, and paints in pallid colours. A few degrees less than dark and subject to my being misled by it.'

The sergeant held his ball-point poised. 'And the time?'

'Ah.' He showed signs of embarrassment, his eyes wobbling. 'I really do apologize, dear boy. I was shaken, considerably so. I am not accustomed to finding dead men in my humble shelter. I needed to recover and in resting I'm afraid I fell asleep. In the High Street car park if you wish to make a note of it.'

'The time, Mr Lockersbie.' Resting, Llewellyn accepted, was a euphemism for Lockersbie's legs collapsing under him.

'I do not at present possess a watch, but I recall hearing the Town Clock striking one.' He paused, thinking it out. 'Or, it occurs to me, it could have been the quarter hour.'

Llewellyn shook his head reprovingly. 'If it was one o'clock, that's over four hours ago. Which isn't very helpful, is it?' He lifted the telephone receiver and dialled a three-figure number, asking for Detective Sergeant Simpson and then speaking in a lowered voice to him.

Lockersbie had taken advantage of the sergeant's detachment from him and moved sideways out of his sight even as he searched in his coat for the bottle. When he reappeared at the end of Llewellyn's conversation his attitude was conspiratorial, his eyes directionally disorganized.

'Cerberus,' he whispered, breathing wine fumes. 'Cerberus was with me.'

'Cerberus?' Llewellyn echoed, staring at him. 'Who's Cerberus?'

'Echidne's dog of doom, dear boy. It's her way of telling me that my miserable days are numbered.' He sounded not too unhappy about it.

'You mean that black dog you say follows you about?' He put down his pen slowly, his earlier conviction of the old man's certainty of having seen a dead man flown out of the window, believing now that the poor old sod had been hallucinating again. 'I've sent a Detective Sergeant to the churchyard on your say-so, Mr Lockersbie,' he said sorrowfully, 'and if he doesn't find anything I'm going to look a right bloody twit.' He smiled, despite feeling gritty-eyed, woollen-brained and nicotine-deprived. 'Take a seat and we'll wait and see.'

As he turned back to his papers he said to himself, 'God help me. Six o'clock coming up and I'm saddled with a dead man, a black dog nobody can see and an amiable lunatic who's going to fall flat on his face any minute.' Even a negative search by Simpson would mean an Occurrence Book entry and a report of

Action Taken and By Whom before he could think of leaving for his bed.

2

On the few occasions that Detective Superintendent George Rogers spent a full night in bed, he got out of it at seven o'clock, showered, shaved and dressed in a sober grey suit, fried his breakfast, ate it, then smoked his pipe and read the doom and depression of his newspaper over three cups of coffee. In this way, he faced the new day with a fragile amiability and an evanescent optimism.

He slept alone and prepared his own breakfast because his wife had left him. As a sufferer from a duodenal ulcer might, he had grown used to the pain of her departure and it no longer kept him awake at night. Like most other wholly masculine men he had unwelcome and unsettling periods when imagery filled his mind with women's mouths and scented breasts. Of this he disapproved, considering that it fitted ill with his Detective Superintendent persona and interfered with a thinking that should be concentrated on the mechanics of eliminating villainy. He made the mistake of fighting it and his psyche suffered.

Black-haired, swarthily complexioned and wedge-nosed, his dark brown eyes uncompromising with a policeman's discomfiting stare, he was no man, even at his most genial, to slap heartily on the back. But if his expression was not amiable, neither was it forbidding, holding it as he did in a neutral impassivity.

At nine o'clock to the minute he would enter his Headquarters office, sit in the black executive-type chair at his desk, unlock the drawers and light up a fresh pipe of tobacco. On his blotting-pad – its paper replenished daily in blue by his secretary whether he had used it or not – would be six *Night Crime Reports* from the Divisions. Before doing anything else he would read them, informing himself of what the local world of villains, their victims and those who had got away with it had been up to while he slept, for his rank allowed him a night's remoteness from any crime deemed of less than major dimensions.

At nine-thirty his second-in-command, Detective Chief Inspector David Lingard – were he not otherwise investigating a crime – visited him to sit in conference.

Lingard was an anachronistic man, a carry-over from the eighteenth century. Being unmarried and able to afford it, he was a contemporary Beau Brummel in elegant smooth tweeds with a collection of dandified embroidered waistcoats and silk shirts high in the collar and long on cuffs. To go with them he had narrow patrician features, blond hair worn a little too long for a policeman and intimidatingly blue eyes which could warn offered violence that to go further might be dangerous. He used snuff in his aquiline nose and carried with him its perfume of attar of roses.

He sat with Rogers now and, because the day promised heat, was without a waistcoat. Rogers, who envied him his shirts but could never discover who made them, considered that waistcoatless he looked incomplete, half-naked.

'You've seen this business about old Lockersbie, David?' he asked, regarding him over a bowl of flowers also placed there by his secretary who, he suspected, had her mind set on narrowing the occupational gap between them to a less professional intimacy. He worried occasionally that she would find him one day in a trough of non-resistance.

'Yes. You're not very happy about it?'

'I'm not satisfied we can write it off so easily as Sergeant Simpson has tried to.' It was evident that Rogers was displeased with the sergeant.

'No,' Lingard agreed. 'But finding no body – no black dog either, if it comes to that – I suppose he had some justification.'

'I don't know much about hallucinations, but it seems to me

there's a big difference between seeing pink elephants or black dogs and seeing a rather ordinary-looking dead man occupying your sleeping patch. They aren't of a kind. I know the poor old chap rabbits on about this dog that follows him and we know it doesn't exist outside his own imagination, but it's a bit of a jump backwards to hallucinate a fairly nondescript body dressed in a very ordinary suit.'

Lingard twitched his mouth. 'I've done the dirty on you, George. I looked up hallucinations in Conybeare's *Textbook of Medicine* before I came in. You may, apparently, imagine seeing quite ordinary blokes sitting on the most ordinary of chairs and the like.'

'But not with black dogs on their laps,' Rogers said drily.

'No, but he was obviously well tanked-up at the time; a man, no doubt, with advanced brain and liver damage and in a condition to imagine anything. I think he's fortunate that so far he only suffers hallucinations.'

'He's also a man of considerable education and culture, David. And, although it doesn't necessarily follow, highly intelligent with it. Until we prove differently, I'm going to accept that he saw what he said he did. It's too easy to dump it by saying he was drunk.' Rogers was slightly censorious. 'I don't doubt that he was, but he could still see, even if his interpretation of what he saw might be faulty. So, it poses interesting questions. Was the man he saw actually dead? If he was, how did he die? Who was he? What was he doing in a church porch at one o'clock in the morning? Why wasn't he still there when Simpson checked five hours later? If he was moved, why and where to?'

'Of course,' Lingard said, not at all seriously, 'he could have gone there under his own steam. Believing he was about to die and like an elephant crawling off to the right place to do it.'

'And burying himself when he did?' Having made up his mind, Rogers became brisk. 'First things first, David. We'll check on the Missing Persons files and . . .'

'I've done so.' Lingard reached and handed him a printed form. 'I anticipated you. The only missing male for the past two days, and with a bit of loose thinking he could fit.'

'I thought you disagreed with me?'

'Devil's advocate,' Lingard murmured. 'It pleases me to bring out the bastard in you.'

'When was this reported?'

'Shortly before nine. It's hot from a typewriter.'

Rogers read aloud. *'Richard Francis Knostig, 44 years, 5' 10", medium build. Dark brown hair, thinning at temples; clean shaven; hazel eyes; small scar left corner of mouth. Dress: navy-blue blazer, grey twill trousers, blue shirt and tie, black shoes. In possession of Lloyds cheque book, Cashpoint and Credit Cards, about £80 in notes. Left home at Nympton Manor, Spye Green, at 2 p.m. 16th August. Driving Citroën Safari blue Estate, index RFK6HH. No known reason for not returning. In good health. Reported by telephone by Mrs Olivia Knostig, 8.50 a.m. 18th August. Action taken: hospital admissions checked, nil result. Circulated Divisions for information only.* H'm,' Rogers sounded cautious, not committing himself. 'You can't very well call a blazer and grey trousers a suit.'

'Seen in the moonlight, George, and that can mean anything.'

'You may be right. Except that his wife took her time about reporting him missing, the rest of it tells us nothing very much. Nothing about whether he's had a screaming row with her, is suicidal, mad-brained or knocking around with another woman; any of the reasons why people decide they've had enough of marriage.'

'So you think him a possibility?' Lingard withdrew a tiny ivory box, tapped it with his forefinger and inhaled snuff, flicking away loose grains from his nostrils with a crimson silk handkerchief.

'He's the only one we've got, David, and Spye Green's not that far from the church. Do you know anything about him?'

'I know the house. Never been in it, but I understand they keep butterflies. Or breed them, I'm not sure which. You can see masses of netting cages in the gardens. They don't care much for visitors, for I've heard that the gates are mostly locked.'

'For which I don't blame them these days. They just may not wish their stuff to be vandalized. What about any women missing? Is there one he's likely to have gone off with?'

Lingard, used to this dodging around technique of questioning, was prepared for it. 'Two,' he answered, 'and both highly unlikely. One's an old lady with high blood pressure and alopecia who goes off regularly each month; the other a twenty-year-old who's believed to have skipped with a fellow punk rocker. Bright orange hair, a red stripe down her nose and safety-pins all over.' He shook his head. 'Not, I understand, very fragrant or the likely choice of a man with a Citroën Safari and a manor house.'

'You'd be surprised,' Rogers said cynically. 'Orange hair and a nose stripe needn't put him off in the dark. Although,' he added reflectively, 'the safety-pins might.' He pushed aside the interesting thought. 'Which is all speculation. You and I will visit the church and see what is what. Then I'll make my number with Mrs Knostig and get a photograph of her husband. You in the meantime can find friend Lockersbie and return with him here. Try and dry him out sufficiently for him to be able to look at it when I return. I have,' he said with the air of a hound catching the scent of a fox, 'a nasty feeling that we have a murder on our hands.'

3

Tar patches in the road were softening and hot air shimmering mirages from its distant surfaces when Rogers braked his car to a halt outside the church.

On the outskirts of the town, it stood grey-stoned and

high-towered in an Edwardian residential area of pink-brick houses with tall windows, heavy on walled gardens, shaven lawns and Virginia creeper; thick with well-endowed widows living on their own and brandy-complexioned men and their wives who could afford the time to play weekday golf.

A short yellow-gravelled path flanked by a yew hedge led to the porched door shadowed from the sun and screened from the road. A notice board stood at the entrance giving in gold on black the times of services and naming the officiating rector as the Reverend J. J. Gathercole. In the foreground of the church were decaying stone tombs and life-sized marble angels, all now leprous with lichens.

Rogers and Lingard stood together in the porch and looked at it. Apart from its large varnished double door with a black iron latch and hinges, a flagstoned floor and a narrow arched window on each side, there was nothing, no obvious signs of its occupancy by either Lockersbie or a dead man.

Rogers said 'H'm', because there was little else to say in the face of an empty porch clean of dust or debris, with not even a blown-in leaf or a discarded cigarette packet to examine. At first sight it was a negation of Locard's Exchange Principle, which was always the cornerstone of Roger's thinking. Where two objects had been in contact – in this instance a dead body and a stone floor – each must necessarily transpose some of its material, gross or microscopic, on to the other. He knew it had to be so, despite appearances to the contrary, and he stooped to scrutinize the flagstones more closely, touching the surface worn smooth by countless church-going shoes.

'Have a scenes-of-crime man brush up in here, David,' he said. 'There might be clothing fibres. And there's a tiny spot of something near the door sill that can be soaked off.'

'It isn't blood.' Lingard squinted at it. 'Too transparent. Probably old man Lockersbie dribbling his wine.' He was going along with his senior, but not all the way. He didn't yet share wholly Rogers's nasty feeling of murder committed.

'Could be. We don't even know where the body was supposed to be lying.' Rogers straightened his legs with a grunt. Sweat was beginning to dampen his shirt collar. 'In a church porch and obviously waiting to be disposed of. Along comes Lockersbie and he interrupts what's going on. But only interrupts, because when Simpson gets here hours later the body's gone. So where does one normally dispose of dead bodies, David?'

'Good thinking, George,' Lingard said with mock admiration. 'We'll dig 'em all up and check.'

Rogers scowled. Sometimes Lingard's flippancy scraped at his amiability, particularly so now when he might be proved to be wasting his and Lingard's highly-paid time on the chimera of an old drunk, and might possibly be made to look a gullible idiot.

'Yes,' he said touchily. 'You take the left side of the graveyard and I'll take the right. If I were needing to hide a dead body, I think a recent burial might be the answer.'

The ground at the rear of the church was well tended with its grass mown, although plants around its stone-walled perimeter had been allowed to grow profusely. Between the dark yew trees, tall foxgloves and papery poppies dappled the shadows with colour. Flower-beds of shrub roses and geraniums lined the central path. It was a quiet sanctuary taken over by birds and animals as well as the dead, and Rogers saw the flicker of two cats moving in the shrubbery, timid enough to be feral.

The graves were close together and, as he soon discovered, in no chronological or any other order. Walking briskly past the long-time dead and those more recently concealed under green or brown chippings, he found it in the last row, so modestly inconspicuous that he could have missed it. A long and narrow mound with turves neatly covering it, a single spray of white flowers at its head. There was no mourning card, no indication of who was buried there.

He crouched and inserted his fingers between turves, lifting one and seeing that the roots of the grass had not yet knitted into the soil beneath. Not knowing how long they took to effect anchorage, it didn't tell him anything. The grass on one side was more flattened than on the other and there were small spillages of soil around the mound. They looked fresh, but if there were a means of confirming it he hadn't heard of it. Wishful thinking could take it as a disturbance if the burial were not so obviously recent. If – and Rogers was fast considering it less of a certainty – a body had been placed there, its equivalent mass in earth would have to be removed and somehow concealed. Were that not to be found it would mean a further diminishment of his shrinking certainty.

Lingard, having covered his area of search and rejoining him, said, 'We've company, George. And looking hot under his dog-collar.' He indicated the man striding purposefully towards them.

Wearing a cream linen jacket and dark-grey trousers with his dog-collar, he had to be the Reverend Gathercole. Rogers cursed his remissness in not first making his number with him before intruding in his air space.

Gathercole appeared also to think that he should have for there was an air of held-back hostility about him. 'Good morning,' he said, without seeming to think it was. 'Is there anything I can do to help you?' He was a plump smooth man with sandy hair and eyebrows; a man, Rogers thought, likely to put the fear of hell into old ladies and choirboys and having the arrogance of certainty written all over him.

Rogers smiled, disarmingly he hoped. 'Good morning. I'm Detective Superintendent Rogers and this is Detective Chief Inspector Lingard. You are Mr Gathercole?'

'Yes. You look like a policeman, which is why I came over.' He waited, obviously for more.

'I was going to get in touch with you,' Rogers said, recognizing heavy going when he met it, 'but I didn't know where you lived.'

'I saw you from my study window, so finding me wouldn't have been so difficult. Are you looking for something?'

'More or less. You had a homeless man wandering around in

here last night who insists he saw a dead man in your church porch.'

'Did he indeed?' The sandy eyebrows lifted. 'And *is* there a dead man?'

'I don't know. Certainly not obviously so at the moment.' The detective had lost the initiative and was himself being interrogated. 'Which is why we've been searching.' He was conscious of Lingard behind him, no doubt silently enjoying his discomfort.

'I could have told you that, superintendent, had you asked me,' Gathercole said pointedly. 'I took an early service this morning.'

'If there was a dead man in your porch he would have been removed before then. Possibly . . .' He indicated the grave between them. 'Possibly concealed in something like this. It's the only one in which it's reasonably likely.'

The eyebrows went up again. 'You can't be serious. One of my parishioners is buried there.'

'How long ago?'

Gathercole frowned. 'If it is relevant, last week. And the grave is exactly as I last saw it.'

'Who was it?'

'A Mr Harland.' He gestured impatiently with a plump hand. 'This is absolute nonsense, superintendent.'

'So it might be,' Rogers said, mildly enough. 'So many of the complaints we investigate are. But it has to be done.' He gave him a brief account of Lockersbie's allegations, without naming him or indicating his custom of sleeping in the church porch. He had the feeling that Gathercole would disapprove strongly of it.

'And you believe this, ah, rather disreputable man?' He obviously did not and there was an edge of derision in his voice.

'No more, no less, than I believe every complaint, say, of rape or false pretences,' he said patiently, although the rector was beginning to nettle him, endorsing as he was his own growing uncertainty. Broad daylight and a hot sun played havoc with intuitive hunches. 'But we do nevertheless have to consider them and do something. In this case, such as checking whether the body might have been buried on top of your parishioner.'

'Which I believe, superintendent, to be a quite unwarranted assumption on your part.'

'It won't offend Mr Harland if it is. But for me, given the need to conceal a body it's a likely place.'

Gathercole frowned again. 'Mine is the authority here and you haven't convinced me of anything. This ground is consecrated to God and to disturb it without the sanction of the Church is a blasphemy.'

'Which is what may have happened already, Mr Gathercole. Dammit,' he said tersely, 'I find your attitude most unhelpful. I don't wish to disinter your parishioner – I'd apply for an Exhumation Order if I did – merely to check beneath the turves. You can provide your own grave digger to do it if you think we're likely to contaminate them. And I'll see to his payment. Is that too much to ask?'

Rogers had offended him further with his brusqueness. 'Yes, it is,' he said stiffly, his face reddening.

'Then I'll ask someone else. I imagine there must be a someone else?' He saw in Gathercole's eyes that there was and also that he did not particularly like policemen. 'Is there?' he pressed him.

'Yes,' he answered reluctantly. 'But I doubt on the evidence you have given me that permission would be forthcoming.'

'That'll be my problem, Mr Gathercole. Who?'

'If you insist. The legal authority is the Chancellor of the Diocese, the Official Principal and Vicar-General.'

'Where do I find him?'

'His address is care of the Ecclesiastical Registrar and he is Mr Bloss the solicitor, whom you will, I'm sure, know.'

Rogers did. Bloss would release authority as willingly as he would the balance of his bank account. 'Thank you,' he said conciliatorily. 'I understand your objections and I hope you understand the necessity for my having to insist.'

If the rector did, it wasn't showing on his features. They in silence, each willing the other to go, until Rogers said, 'I'm not going to disturb anything, but I'd like to look around again before I go.'

Gathercole turned without a word and left them, Rogers certain that he would be on the telephone as soon as he could, complaining to somebody about meddlesome and objectionable police officers and also watching them from his study window as potential body-snatchers.

'You're asking to be excommunicated, George,' Lingard said, 'or whatever it is the clergy do to blasphemers.'

'An occupational risk, and I'll survive. In his position, I don't blame him for not going along with us. It seems a fairly respectable church to have dead bodies dumped in its porch.' Rogers didn't like bulldozing over people, but not even the Established Church was going to be allowed to interpose itself between him and the unmasking of villainy. 'Let's look at the flower-beds and see if they tell us anything.'

The beds had been neatly tended and were apparently weed-free. Soil could have been spread on them, its surface dried of dampness by the sun and rendered virtually indistinguishable from the original covering. Crouching and sifting it through his fingers, Rogers found beneath it a tiny seedling with two leaflets, green enough to have once seen daylight, its roots still firmly embedded. It could have been covered by the gardener, but he didn't think so and he was satisfied. His certainty returned, his earlier belief in Lockersbie justified.

'I'm going to be right, David,' he said matter-of-factly over his shoulder. His adrenalin had not yet started pumping. It needed an actual dead body to do that, but he felt its promise.

Lingard, pinching snuff into his nostrils and agreeing with him, having made his own assessment, murmured, 'Who could ever doubt it?'

On the way out, identifying the rectory on the opposite side of the road, Rogers waved a friendly hand at the Reverend

Gathercole watching them from a ground-floor window. Amiability to a man whom he believed was going to lose out wasn't difficult.

4

Rogers, idling in an exhaust-smoking traffic queue and using up expensive petrol on the way to Spye Green, only partly mollified by his getting an official mileage allowance, felt frustrated and, but for Lingard, solitary in a world of doubters.

Having returned his second-in-command to Headquarters, he had called at the office of Bloss and had been given a less than fifteen-minute audience with him: an austere and shrewd lawyer advantageously entrenched behind his desk and bundles of intimidating legal documents. The Reverend Gathercole had obviously been in touch with him, for he showed all the held-back impatience of a man listening to something about which he already knew.

While Rogers waited in the queue, his engine overheating, breathing in carbon monoxide and tobacco smoke, he recalled their conversation. 'Very interesting, superintendent,' Bloss had said drily. 'While I cannot dispute, even although it is based on the evidence of an admitted alcoholic, the existence of a dead man, your guess – it can be no more than that – of his being buried in Mr Harland's grave does not, I fear, hold legal water.'

'You mean you are refusing me the authority to look?' Rogers asked. Their personas had already clashed, although the clash was concealed by a civilized politeness.

'My dear chap, certainly not. It just isn't within my power to give it to you. That is for the Chancellor of the Diocese and it requires a formal request.'

'Which I am now making, Mr Bloss.' As Rogers had anticipated, the lawyer was being legalistically rigid, and he suspected that in this office, heavy with the lost hopes of previous supplicants, he wasn't going to get very far.

'Quite so, and I have no option but to forward it. But I am also obliged to make my own recommendation. Which,' he added, 'must be adverse to your application.'

'And how long will all this take?'

Bloss had shrugged. 'Two or three days if the Chancellor is available. More, naturally, if he is not.'

'I don't have that time to wait. I'm having to treat this matter as a murder enquiry and, as you well know, the body will be needed for identification and a post-mortem examination. It won't help, it won't be in anyone's interest, in its having been buried for days. Bodies do decay, you may recall.'

'So they do, superintendent,' Bloss countered, politely obdurate. 'Produce some acceptable evidence that there is a body there and I assure you that there will be no difficulty.'

And that, after further unavailing pressures by Rogers, was as far as he had been able to get. It strengthened his belief that too many lawyers obstructed justice, too few worked for it. For all that, he was going to look the bloodiest of bloody idiots if the body was not where his reasoning told him it had to be.

With the traffic once more moving, though at a tortoise-like crawl, and the sun parboiling a frustrated Rogers, he shrugged aside any doubts that might inhibit his investigation. In interviewing Mrs Knostig he had a problem. Missing persons did not call for police action, least of all a visit by a Detective Superintendent, unless the circumstances suggested a likely fatal outcome or that the going missing was connected with a crime. Adults of sound mind were free to leave home, desert wives or husbands should they choose to do so, without its being any business of the constabulary. He could not in this instance tell Mrs Knostig that possibly her missing husband was decomposing (and more rapidly in the summer's heat than he could wish for) in another's grave. He thought about him lying there, looking up at the underside of turves with soil in his mouth and waiting to be uncovered; he felt sorry for him, and worried on his own account that this was a day beginning to fit badly within his skull.

The large wrought-iron gates, needing a coat of paint and denying access to the high-walled gardens of Nympton Manor, were not locked, but the small notice NO ADMITTANCE would be off-putting to casual visitors. Refusing to admit that it might apply to him, Rogers opened them, noticed that they also needed oiling, and drove through, having to get out to close them again and not allowing it to irritate him.

The drive needed regravelling and what were once spacious lawns had been let grow to lush and seeding grass. On them, between straggly cupressus and rhododendron bushes with dead flower heads, were large hooped structures covered with green netting; inside, seen indistinctly, the foliage of shrubs. By them was a creosoted wooden-slatted shed, as out of place on the lawn as the cages.

Although not Rogers's idea of a manor, the house was large and old enough to have its mushroom-coloured sandstone walls covered with creeper which, allowed to run rampant, had invaded the sills and sides of the lofty windows whose white paint was blistered and flaking. The door at the top of a short flight of steps matched them, its brass knocker tarnished.

He pressed the bell-push at its side and listened. When he heard neither its buzzing nor any movement he banged hard with the knocker, enough to shake the door.

The young woman who opened it gave him an overall impression of brownness. Her hair, cropped and carelessly loose, was black; her plum purple eyes contrasted with the clear whites. The pale olive skin and high cheekbones gave her the appearance of what he imagined a Coptic priestess to be. Thin and fragile-seeming, she wore a loose-fitting dress patterned intricately in shades of brown. She was a woman who made men feel big and masculine and Rogers was no exception.

'Mrs Knostig?' he asked.

'No. You wish to see her?' Her accent made her unmistakably educated and cultured English.

'Please. In connection with her husband.' He produced his warrant card and held it out for her to read. 'Detective Superintendent Rogers.' It had the not uncommon effect – which usually irritated him – of producing in her eyes the shadow of apprehension of his being the bearer of bad news.

She left him standing in the hall to wait, reflecting that – depending on her relationship with the Knostigs – she must be an unsettling character to have around, for she gave off, unmistakably for him, a strong aura of sensuality; a woman with a fire burning inside her.

The furnishings of the hall and those he could see through a door opening into a sitting-room were expensively comfortable but untidy and grossly neglected by polish and dusting cloth. The brown woman was gone long enough for him to suck thoughtfully on his empty pipe and to evaluate what he had seen outside and inside. There was – or had been – money here, and now too much or not enough of it to bother with external appearances; or the occupants too busy or too idle. Nothing of which told him anything.

Putting his head briefly around the sitting-room door, he could smell the wet-dog odour of cigar smoke which, he thought, should not stay around too long in a room with its windows opened. And from what he saw of it, it looked lived in, untidily so. Newspapers left on the chair arms, books in unorganized piles on tables beside them, two empty coffee beakers and plates with cake or biscuit crumbs on them. He was too far away to read the titles of the books but the newspapers were the *Times* and the *Guardian*. Domestically, it would drive Rogers to despair, but he wasn't the absent Knostig who might have had different ideas about living in dust and disorder.

When the brown woman returned he was where she had left him, examining with intent interest the detail of a Dutch flower painting. 'I'm sorry to have kept you waiting,' she said. 'Will you come with me?'

He followed behind her, smelling the fragrance of her scent, conscious of her sensuality and seeing from where her dress touched her body that she might have next to nothing on beneath it. All of which, he considered, was unfair to any married man whose wife had left him.

She led him into a room at the end of the hall, a room which at first glance seemed filled with wooden work-benches crammed edge-to-edge with small netting-covered cages, and with a glass gazebo greenhouse in a corner filled with tall plants and illuminated with strip lighting. What appeared to be large moths fluttered clumsily in the white brilliance. Small plastic trays containing their corpses were on the bench near it, together with a binocular microscope, racked laboratory phials, difficult-looking books, and glass jars filled partly with chopped-up leaves. Frames of pinned butterflies and moths covered the larger part of the walls. Even his brief glimpse of the room made him dislike what it was obviously used for. However it might be rationalized, it was an abattoir for moths and butterflies. In addition to the laboratory equipment there were two wooden chairs and a roll-top desk with a typewriter and a stack of filing drawers on it. Unlike the living-room, here was neatness, order and an absence of dust.

The woman standing near one of the windows had turned as he entered. She was tall and well built without being fat; touching, he judged, on forty and wearing a woollen skirt in disregard of the heat, her blue linen shirt well filled with shoulders and arms but short on breasts. Her hair was a fading yellow, strained back behind her head and tied in a knot as though she didn't care how it looked just so long as it was out of the way, her eyes a cool grey and direct as they took in the detective. A gold-rimmed lens hung by a black cord from her neck. She looked not the sort of woman to wear jewellery or to be seen carrying a handbag. There was a hardness in her features militating against her being a woman Rogers would want on the other side of his newspaper at breakfast. Not, he thought, a female likely to be found on the softer shores of love.

'You've found him?' she asked without preamble and without any visible anxiety either.

'No,' he said, 'I'm sorry. I called to see if there was any further information you might have to help me do it.'

'Of course. Why not?' Her voice was crisp and authoritative. 'I wish Miss Blandford to stay. She may be able to help.'

The brown woman who was Miss Blandford gave him a half-smile, her first, and it showed him beautifully white teeth.

He smiled back. 'I'd be grateful,' he said, although he wasn't. Awkward questions that trod on marital eggshells were best asked and answered alone.

Mrs Knostig didn't ask him to sit and remained standing herself, an indication that his questioning was destined to be limited. He said, 'The constable taking the details from you left a few questions unasked and what we have isn't enough to give our enquiries the weight they deserve. Have you checked to see whether your husband took his shaver and tooth-brushes?'

'I haven't checked, but I'm sure he hasn't. I would have noticed.'

'Or any clothing?'

'I'm certain not. I would have seen.'

'Has he missed returning home before?'

'No.' She had hesitated, almost imperceptibly.

Cynical enough to believe that he could guess one reason for her husband's non-return, Rogers knew they were pointless questions, but they were necessary if she were not to suspect she might already be widowed. He cursed silently the obstructive Gathercole and Bloss.

'Where was he going when he left here?'

'I don't know. He left immediately after lunch and I assumed he would be going into town.' She shrugged. 'The library, shopping, something unimportant enough not to be worth mentioning.'

'An odd question, Mrs Knostig, but it might help.' He hoped

that she wouldn't guess that the contents of the stomach might help in determining when and where he had died. 'What did he eat? For his lunch, I mean.'

She stared at him in surprise. 'I do find it odd. Why do you ask?'

'It's routine. You never know when it might come in useful,' he said enigmatically, realizing that it wouldn't convince her and wishing now he had not asked.

She was thinking it out and unable apparently to find a reason for refusing to tell him. 'I can't see how it could. If you really have to know, we had cheese, a duck pâté and water biscuits. And some white wine,' she added.

'Thank you. He left almost two days ago, Mrs Knostig, a full two nights. Isn't that a longish time to decide on reporting him missing?'

She tightened her lips. 'Are you reproving me?'

'No, merely trying to find out why.'

'I have my sufficient reasons.'

'He doesn't go to an office or whatever?' She was making it difficult for him. Whoever said that women were the gabby sex hadn't met Mrs Knostig.

'No. Not even whatever.'

'Can you tell me what he does?'

'As you've no doubt already observed, this is a butterfly and moth breeding and research centre. My husband is a lepidopterist and he started this as a commercial enterprise to subsidize its aims in conservation and, later, in experimental genetics.' She added drily, 'I doubt that any of this has anything to do with his disappearance.'

'It would be difficult to imagine it.' Somehow, the thought of any rival butterfly breeder building up enough professional animus to commit murder failed to carry conviction. 'Have you a recent photograph of him? It would help.'

She spoke to the brown woman who had remained standing behind a Rogers acutely aware of her presence, sensing her eyes on him. 'Would you get it, Helen, please.' When she had gone from the room, she said, 'I don't wish you to publish it, to put it on posters. He isn't a wanted criminal.'

He had the impression that she now wished she had not reported her husband's absence to the police. 'I'd no intention of doing so,' he assured her. 'Just being missing wouldn't justify it.' Taking advantage of Helen Blandford's absence he was about to dig in, but to choose his words carefully. 'I hope that you will be frank with me, Mrs Knostig. Men don't usually leave home without there being some underlying cause. Not in good health and with no problems. It may be something you feel to be embarrassing, but I assure you that I've heard it all before.' He held her stare unblinkingly. '*Was* there something?'

She turned her head away from him, looking through the window. Even in that there was a touch of arrogance. 'I'm afraid I was less than honest when I spoke on the telephone. You would understand, Mr Rogers.' That wasn't a question but a statement on which she assumed agreement.

'It's why I asked you with Miss Blandford out of the room.'

'You need not have waited,' she said ungraciously. 'Miss Blandford is well aware of the situation. My husband drinks excessively for his particular temperament. It has led to un-pleasant arguments, a lack of communication on his part.' He couldn't see her expression but her voice sounded bleak. 'Which is how he could leave the house without telling me why. Which is why I delayed reporting him as missing.'

'He's an alcoholic?'

'No,' she said sharply, 'not at all. He has a low level of tolerance to it. Even you must see that there's a difference.'

'Had there been an argument before he left?'

'If it is any business of yours, yes. And no, I don't propose discussing it with you.'

'You mentioned his temperament, and I have to ask you this. Would you think him suicidal?'

She jerked her head back to meet his gaze. 'Good God, no!' She was scornful. 'What an absurd suggestion to make.'

He was beginning to believe that she had a mouth like a

paper shredder and that he kept putting his hand into it. 'So many of us do absurd things, Mrs Knostig,' he said, mildly for him and not prepared to take offence. 'Would there be any question of a loss of memory?'

There was again a barely perceptible pause that indicated she was thinking. 'It's a possibility,' she conceded. 'There has been an occasional amnesia, forgetting names and things, but that's not the same, is it?'

'No. What about friends, associates, other relatives who might be able to throw some light on where he's gone?'

What he sought and did not yet intend asking was the possibility of a mistress or two, or a discovered goating after the very delectable (and, he thought, therefore very dangerous) Helen Blandford, although he wasn't certain whether excessive alcohol inflamed or dampened sexual ardour.

Her chin lifted and she glared at him with her grey eyes. 'I hope that you don't intend making this more public than it already is.'

'You mean you're refusing?'

'I most certainly am.'

'I do have an obligation to your husband as well,' he pointed out.

'So you may, but I intend not to be further embarrassed.'

He sighed. She was resenting his questioning and he couldn't blame her. Given her belief that her quarrelsome husband had fled the coop, he would feel the same if a stranger were to poke his inquisitive nose into the reasons for his own wife leaving him. The more pertinent and insistent questions could come later when he had a dead body to prop up the more demanding aspect of his authority.

The door, left ajar, opened and Helen Blandford entered the room, a framed photograph in her hand. She had been a long time getting it and he had not heard her returning, giving him the feeling that she could have been listening outside. She showed the photograph to Mrs Knostig who nodded, then handed it to Rogers.

It didn't tell him much. Knostig looked a solid enough citizen in dark-rimmed spectacles; a man who could be met twice in a bar and not remembered the third time. His unexceptional features had nothing in them to suggest a weakness for alcohol or women, or to mark him out as a murder victim. Nor did he look the sort of man capable of overawing the formidable Mrs Knostig into marrying him. But then, Rogers admitted to himself, he didn't believe that he or most men would be either.

'Yes,' he said to her, 'it will help.' He indicated the work-benches and the laboratory paraphernalia on them. 'He left all this?'

'No. This is my work. My husband is not a geneticist.'

'But you are?'

'Yes.' She appeared to welcome a change of subject. 'I specialize in the hereditary factors of the *Sphingidae*. You probably know them as hawk-moths,' she added with a down-putting air which he felt unearned.

'If they're the ones who eat my old suits, I do,' he said solemnly, overstating his ignorance.

She managed a quick patronizing smile. 'You mean the larvae of the clothes moth; sub-order *Heteroneura*, family *Tineoidea*.'

'If they're the ones with the sharp teeth, yes.' He looked deliberately at the trays containing the dead insects. 'Your research involves killing them?'

'Naturally. Those I need to dissect and study.'

'To what end?'

She sensed clearly the disapproval he had thought he had concealed and lost her brief geniality. 'Knowledge, Mr Rogers,' she said tartly, looking down her nose at him. 'Scientific knowledge.'

'I see. And the butterflies?'

'My husband's side.' She said nothing more, waiting in a shut-off silence. He had gone over the edge of her tolerance for unwanted questions and was being dismissed.

'I'll let you know as soon as I have any information,' he said formally.

Helen Blandford walked with him to the outer door while he fished in his mind for something to say that would establish a communication between them. Her mere presence did things to him and the masculinity behind the policeman's protective coloration was responding.

All he managed to say was, 'I hope my visit hasn't upset Mrs Knostig.'

'I don't think so,' she answered him. He imagined that her eyes held a hostility as though she found him distasteful and he felt snubbed. She held the door open for him and he sensed her gaze following him as he descended the steps into the hot sun, not much wiser now than when he had climbed them.

Driving away, suffering the enclosed heat of the car which brought him out in a sweat, he saw a burly man in green overalls and a check cloth cap watching him from the doorway of one of the cages. Not the sort of man, he thought, to smoke a cigar in the sitting-room of Nympton Manor or to read either the *Times* or the *Guardian* while doing it.

He swore when he had again to go through the performance of opening and closing the gates, in a mood to have left the damned things swung back.

5

Rogers didn't like the new Headquarters building. Outside, it was all featureless concrete and glass in stark unrelieved rectangles; inside, shiny rubber-floored corridors lined with identical doors leading to offices furnished with functional grey metal desks, plastic chairs, steel filing cabinets and typewriters. The reports, forms and files being passed through them and processed dealt at second hand with despairing, angry and frustrated humanity. Nothing of the suffering they reflected was held in the ambience of the building and, in it, Rogers often felt dehumanized and remote from the smells and dirt of villainy in the town outside. It was something he fought against by cultivating a distaste for paperwork.

With the venetian blinds lowered over the opened windows to keep out the sun, his office was less hot than the inside of a pressure cooker but not, he considered, much. His desk was laden with a stack of crime files and reports awaiting his reading and annotating with his directions such as *Prosecute*, *Caution, No further action* or the occasional *Unsatisfactory – continue enquiries*. They would wait there until he decided that they were more important and pressing than the missing Knostig.

Having taken off his jacket and lit a fresh pipe of tobacco, expecting the return of Lingard with Lockersbie, he used the time to make a record in his pocketbook of his interview with Mrs Knostig. Following it, he added notes.

Knostig: House fabric neglected. Financial difficulties? But Citroën Safari, personal number plate, £80 and credit cards. Also gardener employed? Marital problems? Very likely. Check extent of drinking.

Mrs Knostig: Lack of concern for husband. Personal pride? Holding back on information. Why?

Helen Blandford: Position in household? Live in? Relationship professional? Employee? Interview alone.

Cigar smoke: Visitor? Occupant of house? Why no see? Why no mention? Connected HB? Knostig smoke cigars?

With his thirteen years' experience and the £15,000-odd a year he received, he accepted that in any murder enquiry he had to come up with something brilliant, penetrating and wholly successful. So far he had, but re-reading his notes he wasn't inclined to heady optimism about this one. He was tempted to telephone Bloss and to reinforce his earlier arguments with hard words, although he knew it would be a waste of time and could have an opposite effect. His hand was reaching tentatively for the receiver when the bell rang.

His caller was Sergeant Dickerson of CD Sub-Division,

32

reporting that P.C. Forbes on beat patrol had located Knostig's Citroën in the railway station car park. It was locked and, no parking tickets being issued for entrance, gave no indication of how long it had been there. Other than a raincoat and an umbrella in the back, it was empty.

'Instruct Forbes to stay with it, sergeant,' he said, 'and await my arrival. It isn't to be touched by anyone.' He replaced the receiver with a hollow feeling that Knostig might not, after all his theorizing, be the dead man Lockersbie had seen. And now it was *if* he had seen one, for this indication that Knostig had gone somewhere by train had, in its turn, undermined his confidence in there being a dead man at all. His earlier doubts returned full flood, and the clearest thing he saw was the smug and infuriating I-told-you-so smile that would be on Bloss's face. He had stuck his neck out with a vengeance.

'Bloody hell!' he swore aloud. What galled him most was that he had dragged his second-in-command along with him in chasing this very probable *ignis fatuus* of a murder. Was he such a mini-brained and gullible idiot to have accepted at second hand the ramblings of a drunken old man? Seeing substance where there were only shadows?

He was brooding darkly over how he could get out from under with a reasonable amount of dignity when he heard footfalls in the corridor outside, a knock on his door and Lingard entered. He was not looking very happy, which made two of them.

'He's outside,' he said. 'I found him asleep in the library reading room.' He shook his head dolefully. 'I don't think you're going to like it, George, but he says he doesn't remember.'

'That's all I need to make my day,' Rogers growled, scowling. 'Bring him in.'

Lockersbie, wearing his caped overcoat with the shape of a bottle discernible in its pocket and carrying his blanket and stick, lifted his disreputable hat courteously as he came in. He knew Rogers and said 'Dear boy' as he reached across to shake hands. He appeared to be sober, although behind the battered spectacles his eyes wobbled unsteadily.

Seated at Rogers's invitation, he draped the rolled blanket over his knees and beamed amiably at the two detectives.

'Thank you for coming in, Mr Lockersbie,' Rogers said, wondering how he could possibly wear a thick overcoat in the heat of the day and not be suffocated or dehydrated. Whether from that or from his drinking, his complexion was what Rogers would call piglet-pink. He pushed the photograph of Knostig over to him. 'Would you mind looking at this and telling me if you've seen him before?'

The old man held it in a shaking hand, blinking at it. 'No,' he said, pushing it back. 'I don't believe I have.'

'He's not the man you saw last night in the church porch?'

'A man in the porch, dear boy?' he said blankly, then looked at Lingard. 'Your colleague asked me that.'

'I know. I mean the man you told Sergeant Llewellyn was dead. The man you thought was sleeping in your place. You touched him on the shoulder to wake him up and it frightened you. The man you described quite specifically.'

'Did I tell him all that? Oh dear.' He frowned in earnest thought, his fingers plucking at his beard. 'If you say I did . . . naturally, I must have done. But I really cannot remember . . .'

'Perhaps this will stimulate your thinking, Mr Lockersbie.' Lingard held out his ivory snuff box to him. It was an uncommon gesture on the detective's part to anybody with other than immaculate fingers.

'Delighted,' the old man said, taking a pinch and inhaling it with an elegant flourish Lingard must have envied. 'Most civil of you, sir.' He licked his lips as though indicating that a drink too would not come amiss, then turned back to Rogers. 'You said, dear boy, I saw a dead man in my porch?'

'Yes, you told Sergeant Llewellyn,' Rogers repeated patiently, despite a simmering compulsion to stand and sweep everything from his desk before roaring his frustration at nobody in particular. 'At five o'clock this morning. Only seven hours ago.'

Lockersbie shook his head, blinking his helplessness. 'It's gone, I'm afraid. I really do apologize.'

'It doesn't seem possible,' Rogers said with resignation, but he knew it was, for Lockersbie's attitude carried conviction and he would never lie. The wine he drank with such stubborn perseverance must be doing horrible things to his brain if not to his body; and Rogers, taking in his bony emaciation, wasn't too sure even of that.

He spoke to Lingard, his voice revealing nothing of the doubts he felt were now becoming certainties. 'I've to see a man about a car, David, so perhaps you'd take Mr Lockersbie up to the church. It may jog his memory.' Opening a lower drawer of his desk he took out a bottle and two glasses. It wasn't something he wanted to do to an alcoholic, but he knew that the old man was intent on drinking himself into forgetfulness about his dead wife, refusing any help to do otherwise, and he guessed that withdrawal was too late and would be too painful for him anyway. Blocked behind the watery blue eyes was information Rogers needed; confirmation that there had been the body of a dead man, even were it not Knostig's. And what could numb memory cells might also reactivate them.

'The sun's well above the yardarm,' he said to Lingard, 'so, before you go, entertain Mr Lockersbie with whatever he wishes.'

It was never in Rogers to go down without firing off all his cannon, ineffective though they might prove to be. Nor was he certain whether it was stubbornness or bloody-mindedness.

6

Entrance to the railway station car park was governed by a bar which lifted automatically when 40 pence was fed into a machine. Once there, Rogers knew from experience, so far as it appeared to concern the British Rail Authority, a car would rot away before it was noticed. The serried ranks of those now filling it baked in the sun, shimmering heat ripples from enamel and chromium. Rogers, his optimism not yet dead but moribund, had brought with him Detective Sergeant Magnus, a ginger-haired and zealously meticulous scenes-of-crime searcher, equipped with a camera, fingerprint powders and a huge bunch of car keys.

The location of Knostig's car was marked by the conspicuous figure of P.C. Forbes standing patiently by it. He saluted as Rogers approached. The detective took in his neat appearance, his trim haircut and burnished boots and approved, making a mental note to earmark him for a CID secondment. A beat man who could take the trouble to search a car park filled to capacity on the strength of a *Circulation for Information Only* could be worth having in the Department.

He gave him enough confidence to take Knostig's photograph from his briefcase and hand it to him. 'He's the owner of the car, Forbes,' he said. 'Go across to the station and see if anybody remembers him buying a ticket, having it punched or making an enquiry.' It was unlikely, he told himself as Forbes saluted again and left him, but it had to be done, although an identification would put paid once and for all to his over-imaginative theorizing.

He concentrated his attention on the Citroën while Magnus tried his keys in the door lock. (Even a put-together mass of metal, glass and rubber should make a statement about itself if looked at hard enough.) It was middle-aged and dusty with a six-months' tax disc on the fly-specked windscreen. The fat tyres were tread-worn, the brown blisters of body-rot showing on the door sills. The leather of the driver's seat was polished and well indented, the passenger's seat obviously little used. The rear seats had been folded into the floor and the raincoat and umbrella had been thrown together in an untidy heap on them. He considered them articles that any man not a rabid optimist about the weather would take with him on a rail journey. There was nothing about the car to tell him how long it had been standing there.

Magnus said 'Ah,' and pulled the driver's door open. Rogers waited until the interior heat had dissipated, then climbed into the seat. For his own six feet and a bit length it was a little cramped, but it would suit anybody a couple of inches shorter. Because whatever had or had not been handled the steering wheel had to have been, he told the sergeant to dust it first, moving over into the passenger's seat.

Pulling out the ashtray, he found cigarette ends in it. Knostig was probably not a cigar smoker, but only probably not. The document compartment contained an old RAC membership book, a certificate of third party insurance, an MOT test certificate, a driver's licence and a vehicle registration document. In the glove compartment, he found a pair of clip-on tinted lenses and a few ten-pence coins.

Magnus, caressing white powder gently on to the rim of the steering wheel with a squirrel-hair brush, was frowning. 'That's odd, sir,' he muttered. 'There's nothing, not a fragment. And it's not glove-wearing weather either.'

For Magnus, to whom fingerprints found were the gold coins of success, it was a failure; for Rogers, the brazen heat became a friendly warmth, the blue sky bluer and his pipe of tobacco the first he had enjoyed that day.

He knew now that Forbes was wasting police time enquiring at the station, convinced that Knostig had not driven the car himself to the park and, therefore, had not gone anywhere by train. That a somebody else had wiped the steering wheel clean of what must have been his own fingerprints put Knostig, in Rogers's now unshakeable opinion, back under the aegis of Saint Boniface where Lockersbie had said he had seen him.

Before returning to Headquarters, Rogers had checked beneath the flooring of the Citroën as a precaution against somebody being unoriginal enough to have hidden a body there. Finding only a box of tools, he had left Magnus to finish his search for fingerprints and with instructions to sweep up the dust and debris from the car's floor-mats for examination at the Forensic Science Laboratory. Having the time and being on sufficiently agreeable terms with his stomach, he had eaten a mushroom omelette at the Minster Hotel, enjoying both it and the comforting feeling that he might not be so mini-brained as he had been beginning to believe.

In his office, with a hiatus in any useful line of enquiry, he applied part of his thinking to the pile of crime files which had grown during his absence. He was feeling amiable enough to lean towards endorsing *Caution* rather than *Prosecute*, but not enough to dispel his frustration that with Knostig remaining undug he was unable to charge around in hot pursuit of whoever had done whatever had been done to him. Which was the problem.

He knew very little as hard facts, could only assume so much. Any man owning a run-down house and a Citroën Safari with overworn tyres, third party insurance and a half-yearly road fund licence could be assumed to be either recklessly tightfisted or chronically short of money, but neither was an adequate reason for having been found dead in a church porch. Domestically, his situation was not proven; his wife either did not care deeply about his being missing or she was putting a brave face on her distress. Finding out who had driven the car to the station intending it to be assumed that Knostig had caught a train was, he told himself sardonically, going to be simple. Somebody either male or female who might not find it necessary to adjust the seat of the car to drive it; somebody knowing an unprofessional little about the presence of fingerprints, but nothing about the implications of their absence.

He broke up the tediousness of reading the files and his repetitive and unfruitful conjectures about Knostig by reading up references in Archbold's *Criminal Pleading* to dead bodies. He found no support for digging them up on the mere say-so of a suspicious policeman and decided reluctantly that the uncooperative Bloss remained legally correct.

Then, with an unaccustomed indecisiveness, after worrying that the finding of the car might give her false hopes, he telephoned Mrs Knostig. He told her that the car had been found at the station and nothing more, agreeing cautiously with her when she remarked that it appeared her husband had caught a train for his own reasons and would probably return with a quite understandable explanation. She sounded neither elated nor depressed, said 'Thank you, Mr Rogers,' and hung up on him.

P.C. Forbes returned with the photograph, reporting dejectedly that none of the station staff could recall having seen Knostig, relieved but mystified that Rogers appeared to be more pleased with his failure than otherwise.

Lingard, returning and sinking gratefully into a chair, said, 'You should change your sherry, George. As a cure for amnesia it could have been distilled water. He topped it up from his own bottle and it was still no good.'

'It's not important now,' Rogers said, surprising him. He passed on the details of his interview with Mrs Knostig, then told him about the wiped-clean steering wheel. 'That's enough to suggest that something nasty has happened to Knostig, and I'm certain it has.' He looked wryly at his second-in-command. 'I sound as though I'm wishing the poor bugger into being dead instead of missing just to bolster up my own suspicions.' He added, wholly ironical, 'But I have this nagging feeling that if he's dead, if he's been murdered, we should know and perhaps do something about it.'

'Just so long as the poor bugger stays where we hope he is,' Lingard agreed straight-faced.

'Yes, I've thought of that too. Have one of the night-duty P.C.s visit the churchyard. Not to hang around there in case he's seen by Gathercole, but to check each hour on the hour from dusk to dawn. I don't want any body-snatching if the word's got round that we think he's there. And for God's sake tell whoever he is not to . . .'

39

He was interrupted by the telephone bell. 'Mr Rogers?' A woman's voice and he recognized it immediately.

'Yes, Miss Blandford.'

'Mrs Knostig has told me about your finding of her husband's car. Would it be possible for me to see you? I might be able to help.'

'Of course. Where?'

'Would you care to come here this evening? I can't leave the house unoccupied.' She sounded friendly, almost coaxing.

'Will seven-ish be all right?' Her sensuality was being projected in her voice and, somehow, he felt safer with her at the other end of a telephone cable.

'Thank you.'

Replacing the receiver, he said, 'That was the very unsettling Helen Blandford, David, who apparently wants to see me on her own. A *femme fatale* if ever I met one. And she sounded about to confide things.' He was smiling in pretended conceit, adjusting the knot of his tie. 'I hope I don't find the need to wish that I'd borrowed your chastity belt.'

7

With the evening's dying heat sultry and physically enervating, Rogers left the gates of Nympton Manor open. He was conscious enough of the regard of the woman he was to interview to hope that his sweating didn't make him give off the odour of a warm goat.

Answering without delay his banging on the tarnished knocker, she said, 'I hope this isn't inconvenient for you,' and stood aside for him to enter. But not that much aside that he could avoid brushing against her in doing it.

She had changed into a pink silk shirt and a white cotton skirt with leather sandals on bare feet. Manifestly bra-less, her

40

breasts were disturbingly prominent under the shirt. Her hair had been combed into a glossy black cap and she looked not so much a Coptic priestess as a schoolgirl sixth-former just back from a few months roasting her body to a dark tan on a Mediterranean beach; smaller, slighter and more fragile-boned than she had appeared earlier. Rogers liked women with boyish bobs, hoping always that it did not indicate a latent homosexual perverseness.

Closing the door, she led him into the sitting-room and, behind her, he again smelled the fragrance of a lavishly-used scent. It was heady, but not enough to distract him from doing a rapid survey of the room. It was not any more tidy or dust-free than it had been on his morning visit, but the cigar-smoke smell had gone. The coffee beakers and newspapers were as he had seen them, the books on the occasional tables now identifiable as fat doorstop novels.

'Please sit,' she said, 'and take off your jacket if you find it hot. May I offer you a drink?'

He needed one, a long one and salt tablets to go with it, but said, 'No, thank you,' kept his jacket on and settled himself in an overstuffed easy chair that gripped and squeezed him like a giant sponge hand, waiting while she sat herself. Her over-consideration of his comfort made him cautious, suspecting that she wanted something from him.

'You have things to tell me,' he said amiably, 'and I presume Mrs Knostig is out.'

'Yes.' She looked down at the backs of her brown hands. 'I can speak to you in confidence?'

'Not completely. I won't go outside and shout whatever it is from the rooftops, but I'm a policeman, not a priest. I'll use any information you give me where I need to and respect it where it doesn't conflict with my enquiries.'

'I mean, Olivia . . . Mrs Knostig doesn't know that I'm speaking to you. She would be upset . . . terribly.'

'I've never been overly gabby, Miss Blandford, and I'm unlikely to tell her that.' He smiled encouragingly. 'You said

41

you could help me, presumably to find the missing husband.'

'Well . . .' She was hesitant. 'Not exactly that. I wanted you to understand that now he is known to have gone off somewhere by train, Mrs Knostig would like you not to continue trying to find him.'

'She asked you to tell me that?'

'No, but she told *me*. She wouldn't tell you because she knows you would ask why.'

'I would indeed, for he's still missing. So why?'

'I have an awful feeling that I'm being disloyal.' She made a moue and looked down at her hands again.

'Loyalty to a principle is more important than loyalty to a person,' he said. She was making him feel sententious, which he was not. 'If you're going to tell me, Miss Blandford, please do so.'

'I'm sorry, but it is awfully embarrassing for her. She and Richard – Mr Knostig – have not been on the happiest of terms with each other. Separate bedrooms, terrible quarrels, that sort of dismal situation. When he didn't return she was worried that he might do something silly and felt obliged to report to the police, although she doesn't want him back. It's as simple as that.'

'Reporting it is virtually asking us to find him.'

'She thought it a necessary formality and didn't anticipate so much police interest.' She looked him up and down. 'A Detective Superintendent into the bargain.'

He let that pass him by. It wouldn't bear explaining. 'You wish us to drop it?'

'She does.' She smiled at him for being so understanding a man.

'Although it may still be that some harm has befallen him?'

'We are sure that it hasn't, Mr Rogers.'

'But I'm not.' He smiled back at her, taking the abruptness from his words. 'Once we're in motion it's like a man falling from an office block, impossible to stop half way. We do have to satisfy ourselves of his continued well-being. I promise you this, though,' he added, straight-faced. 'If and when we find him I shan't do anything to persuade him to return home.'

'So you're going on with it? Even though Mrs Knostig doesn't wish it?'

'Yes.' He made it very definite. 'And, because I am, I need answers to some questions.'

She was silent for a few moments, measuring him up with her eyes that were clearly calculating, then shrugged her acceptance. 'You can ask them.' An unspoken 'But I may choose not to answer them' hung in the air.

'You said that Mrs Knostig and he were at odds with each other. Why?'

'Who knows?' she said guardedly. 'Marriages don't always work out.'

'Was it connected with his drinking?'

'You should ask *him*,' she said sharply, which meant that it might be.

'Finances?'

'That's being offensively inquisitive.' She drawled that and there was no edge to it.

'Uncomfortable questions often are,' he said easily. 'Were they?'

'I've no intention of answering that.'

'It might be relevant. It so often is.'

When she remained silent he changed course, choosing to get his answers by inference. 'What is your position here, Miss Blandford?'

It surprised her, but she answered him, her chin lifting. 'I'm research assistant to Mrs Knostig. You wish to know my salary?' she asked caustically.

'No. You live in, I assume?' She had no rings on her fingers so he also assumed, for the time being only, that she was neither engaged nor married.

'I do.'

'Which is how you know they don't sleep together?'

'It would be difficult not to know.'

43

'Or does Mrs Knostig confide in you?'

'She doesn't need to. I am not cretinous.'

'Are you on friendly terms with Mr Knostig?'

She stirred uneasily. 'You remind me of a mole digging down in the dirt for worms. And that isn't intended to be complimentary.'

'Which isn't answering my question.'

'No, it isn't, is it?'

He assessed her as a person who would prefer not to answer than to lie. So she also hadn't liked the dead man.

'Is there another woman in the background of the Knostig's marital problems?'

She showed him her glistening white teeth in what was more an expression of disdain than a smile. 'What a sordid mind you have.'

'It's downright filthy,' he said, mocking an apologetic admission. 'I can believe all sorts of nasty things about anybody. Is there another woman? A mistress?'

'Have *you* one?' She showed a trace of amusement.

'Several,' he lied with a grin at her evasive insolence. 'But I don't happen to be missing from home and they aren't relevant. Has he?'

She reached for a packet of cigarettes and lit one, keeping him waiting for her answer. 'If he has, he doesn't happen to have confided in me about her,' she said flatly.

'He must have a friend or two. Even an acquaintance.'

'Of course he has, but I don't have to know of them.' She was weighing him up again, her eyes narrowed through the cigarette smoke, and he found it unsettling. 'But, as it happens, I know of one. Martin Humfries – it's spelt with an "f" – and I really don't know his address. He's an actor, and if you speak nicely to whoever it is at the Beaux Arts Theatre you might be given it.'

'Thank you,' he said drily. 'How friendly?'

Her lips tightened briefly. 'Hadn't you better ask Mr Humfries? He might have a different opinion of it than I.'

He looked through the window into the garden, where the shadows were growing long and the light suffusing into pinkness. 'Is that chap with the cloth cap and overalls I saw lurking out there this morning the gardener?'

'You do dodge around, don't you?' she said. 'Yes, he is. He looks after the food plants. For the larvae of the moths,' she added, seeing the question already poised in his expression. 'They have to eat, they eat a lot and they all have different tastes in what they need.'

'Does he live in, too?'

'Good heavens, no. This isn't an hotel.' He had apparently amused her.

'Have I said something funny?'

'No, not really. It was because he sometimes sleeps in the tool shed. And I don't like him.'

'What's his name?'

'Wimbush. We call him Arthur.' She wrinkled her forehead. 'Do all policemen ask these unnecessary and nosy questions?'

'Probably,' he said unhelpfully. 'Otherwise we wouldn't find out things. Is he also the licensed slaughterman?'

'Slaughterman?' Her mouth opened. 'What on earth do you mean?'

'I mean, does he kill all those moths you seem to need for cutting up into bits?'

'You are being offensive again, Mr Rogers,' she said, but surprisingly mildly. 'Only a few are killed and then quite painlessly. As it's always been done, with crushed laurel leaves in airtight jars, as you probably noticed this morning. And by Mrs Knostig – sometimes Richard – not by Wimbush.'

'If I remember correctly, they produce prussic acid, which doesn't sound painless to me.'

'It's called hydrocyanic acid now,' she corrected him, 'and there is a physiological difference between an insect and a man.' She added, 'You're one of those, are you?'

'Yes,' he agreed, 'I'm one of those.'

She shrugged. 'Even you must have a touch of barbarism.'

45

'Yes, and I restrict it to *Homo sapiens*,' he smiled. 'They can hit back.'

'Can they?' She looked sceptical. 'If it makes you any happier, I don't need to kill my subjects. They don't need cutting up into bits, as you put it. My research for some time now has been the incidence of cannibalism in the larvae of the cinnabar moth and the nocturnal copulation of its imago.'

'That sounds all too much like *Homo sapiens* to me.' He waited for a comment which didn't come, then said, 'I think that's about all I have for the moment, Miss Blandford. But just one other thing. I want to leave the car in the park for a couple of days. I take it Mrs Knostig won't object?'

'I shouldn't think so. She has a car of her own and there's only one key to the Safari anyway. I imagine I shouldn't ask why?'

'You can. Isn't there always the possibility that Knostig may come back and want it?'

'Yes,' she said, 'of course. Silly me.' She tucked her legs on to the chair seat so that the beginnings of her coffee-brown thighs were exposed. Her eyes held his, larger and more luminous and, he thought, sending out messages no male could ever be certain about. 'Can't I persuade you to have that drink? I need one myself after all this grilling.'

If Rogers could change course so, apparently, could she and, probably because she felt she had survived successfully his probing, she was clearly in a more friendly mood. He thought he could accept a drink without bruising his ethics too deeply, for it wasn't as though she were a likely candidate for a pair of handcuffs and an official caution. Cagey and devious she might be, but he believed her honest in her evasiveness. Drinking together was better than sniffing around each other like a couple of suspicious dogs – a dog and a bitch, he corrected himself – and it could provoke a welcome garrulity.

'Thank you,' he said, 'I will. A whisky if you have it.'

She loosened herself from the chair, showing more expanse of thigh as she did it and leaving Rogers to guess whether it was a

46

rather modest and naïve titillation or a careless indifference to what it might do to his libido. He wondered whether the dead Knostig had had such fleshy enticements displayed to him under the nose of his wife.

The drinks were in a cupboard and he watched her as she clinked bottles and glasses pouring them. He stood when she approached him with the glasses and handed him one, a more than generous measure. She stood nearer to him than he thought necessary, her head coming only up to his shirt front, and he felt as though he were standing naked by a red-hot stove.

'*Salud, dinero y amor,*' he said, then, wincing at its probable inappropriateness, sipped the undiluted whisky.

She nodded gravely, not moving away as she drank her own. It left her lips glistening, and Rogers was uncomfortably aware that his hairy-legged, horned and satyric other self was beginning to crawl out from the underbrush of his mind. He mentally cancelled any further questions, drained his glass and looked at his watch. 'I have to go,' he said with what he recognized as utter banality.

'No.' Her face held an odd expression of determination, her eyes dark and intense. 'Is there nothing I can do to persuade you to change your mind?'

'What, about going?' The wearing of brassières by women should be made obligatory, he thought sadly. An imagination of breasts was never so disturbing as having the real things so aggressively prominent a foot or so from itching flesh on a warm evening. And the worst of all temptations was the one to which you couldn't possibly succumb.

'Partly.' She had moved a little closer and he could feel her body heat, the purring vibrations of her sexuality. 'I really do want to convince you that it would be the worst thing for Richard to return here. Can't you just let him stay wherever he has gone? Let him live his own life and not ruin Olivia's? If you really knew . . . *please.*'

He wasn't sure about the intentions of this wholly sensual woman, but if she was intent on seducing him to her interests it was so amateurishly obvious as to be almost pathetic. With a more dangerous directness it had happened to him before with other women. Too-attractive women thieves, the wives and mistresses of villains he had arrested or sought to arrest, even the odd in-debt housewife he had stumbled on by chance earning an afternoon's £10 during her husband's absence. It had never done his ego any good that he should be seen by a woman's fear or need as a man who could be bribed by the casual use of her body.

He made his voice light so that his rejection wouldn't hurt her, pretending a misunderstanding of her intent. 'I'm sorry, Miss Blandford, I really am, but all the talking in the world . . .' he smiled '. . . even another couple of whiskies, couldn't alter it.' He put his glass down and moved away from her towards the door, wanting to break into a brisk trot. 'I'll see myself out if I may.'

She stood there, the glass in her hand, saying nothing and watching him, the saddest thing he had seen that day.

Getting into his car he found himself sweating, and not from the heat now largely gone in the cooling dusk, never giving the closing of the gates a second's thought as he drove away.

8

Propped up on pillows in the dark, proving it a fallacy that if you couldn't see the smoke you couldn't taste, it, Rogers smoked his pipe in bed. It was a satisfaction he had been unable to indulge when his wife also occupied it.

Now it helped his thinking, undisturbed by extraneous distractions like eating a late meal, conferring with Lingard, writing his notes up at his desk and doing other things he felt it necessary to do before finishing for the night. Although now in a more-or-less satisfied mood, he had been less so on his return from the Helen Blandford interview.

Away from her disturbing presence, he accepted that she had told him very little, and her efforts at having a stop put on his enquiries seemed out of all proportion to the prospect of having her employer's missing husband return. He was confident enough to bet money on it – a small amount, he qualified to himself – that Mrs Knostig had gone out by arrangement, leaving Helen Blandford to do the dirty work of wheedling him; that she had been acting under pressure. And none of it had fitted her persona. The only rock-bottom certainty was that neither woman wanted the unloved Knostig back in the house.

He accepted it as a possibility that he had mistakenly assumed the intensity of Helen Blandford's attempted persuasion for sexual seduction, that she had never intended anything other than whisky and sweet words. And, unwilling to do her an injustice, he had not mentioned to Lingard the steamy tail-end of the interview.

Because there were things he had no wish to think about, he put his pipe away and let his brain go off duty; allowing it to drift pleasantly on what might have been had he not been a policeman, had she not been a potential witness in a murder investigation and were she capable of being ignited to passion by a swarthy, six-feet-tall man with black hair and his own teeth. He lost awareness long before that which his fantasizing was leading to actually happened.

It seemed as though he had been asleep for only minutes when the telephone bell reached through to his unconsciousness and woke him. Checking his watch in the moonlight flooding through the window, he saw groggily that it was ten past three. He felt his unlit way downstairs, cursing for the hundredth time his forgetting to plug it into the bedside extension, and lifted the receiver.

'Rogers,' he growled, not yet awake and holding back a yawn.

It was the Headquarters' Duty Chief Inspector. 'Orford

here, sir. Your D.C. Brooker's just radio'ed in to say that he's
found a hand sticking out of a grave at Saint Boniface's Church
and wants you notified immediately.' There was something in
his voice suggesting that he thought Brooker might be certi-
fiable. 'Is he all right, sir? He sounded a bit hysterical, gabbled
on a bit.'

Rogers felt a happy contentment, already organizing what
was working of his brain to what he had to do. 'He's all right,
Mr Orford. He's probably suffering first degree shock. The
owner of the hand was why he was put there.' Now with a
certainty of purpose, he became briskly authoritative. 'When
I've finished with you, get Mr Lingard out of his bed and up
there at his soonest together with my murder box. Advise Dr
Hunter that we have a body and tell her that I'd appreciate her
attendance as soon as it's convenient. Organize floodlights, a
coffin shell, screens, a photographer and a couple of your P.C.s
with strong backs and a spade apiece.'

Dressing, he smiled, thinking out I-told-you-so words he
might get around to saying to Gathercole and Bloss. Because he
would be seeing, if only by moonlight, Dr Bridget Jane Hunter,
pathologist and his quondam lover, he took a few extra minutes
to run a shaver over the bristles on his chin and jowls and rub in
his most expensive after-shave lotion. It contained musk and
was supposed to send women into a hysteria of desire although,
so far, that hadn't been his experience.

9

Moonlight in a churchyard, Rogers accepted, had a disturbing
luminosity that made believable baleful entities in the impenetrable shadows it cast, an eeriness of brooding watchful-
ness emanating from the buried dead. The newer headstones

reflected a phosphorescent light, the older angel-winged figures loomed with a dappled and sinister lividity. The grass was already wet with dew and thick with snails in their nocturnal feeding, the occasional gold glint of cats' eyes watching from the shrubbery. Around was the quietness of a sleeping town. It was a different place from the sun-drenched, bird-singing garden of the previous day and he was glad he was not alone.

Under Rogers's supervision the group of men were active around the grave, the hissing white brilliance of floodlights throwing long shadows that climbed the canvas screens erected on three sides of it. The centre of their interest, a pallid glistening hand, its palm turned upwards with hooked fingers, protruded from the disturbed earth of a scratched-out hole in the turves. It showed a wristwatch and the soil-stained cuff of a blue shirt. The watch, a digital, was still working.

Two P.C.s, their tunics discarded, were lifting turves and scraping away the earth with exaggerated care and no enthusiasm. Rogers, standing monolithic in his waiting patience, smoked his pipe as he watched them. In his amiability at having been proved right, he was addressing the two reluctant P.C.s as Burke and Hare and had changed his mind about using spades for the digging, ordering them to use their hands. The artefact they were excavating like trainee archaeologists needed a delicate touch.

Before sending Brooker to invite the Reverend Gathercole to the disinterment, he had questioned him about his finding of the body. Brooker, wearing an overabundance of down-drooping moustache which, together with the signs of his earlier agitation still on him, was earning Rogers's displeasure, told him that he had visited the grave on the hour from ten o'clock as instructed by Detective Sergeant Simpson. The grave had been undisturbed until his check at three o'clock. He had seen nothing or nobody and no, sir, it hadn't occurred to him to tie a thread of black cotton across the gate to check that nobody had gone in during his absence. Mr Lockersbie hadn't been sleeping in the porch, nor, he was anxiously certain, had it been possible for the Reverend Gathercole to have seen himself entering the churchyard.

Directing his attention again to the grave, Rogers could smell the sickly-sweet stench of putrefaction. Lingard at his side was repeatedly packing his nostrils with snuff against it.

'Providence on our side for a change, David?' he said. 'I wouldn't think that whoever buried him came back to dig him up again.'

'I'm with you.' Lingard had put on a claret-red paisley-patterned waistcoat against the night air and he looked incongruously elegant to be taking part in a Grand Guignol of excavated death. 'Possibly one of the cats? Or a dog?'

'A cat wouldn't be strong enough. A dog or a fox I'd accept. I don't like referring to our dead friend as carrion but a fox would think him so, would sniff him out being so shallowly buried. And a fox digs, more so than a dog.'

'Whatever it was it was sent by God to confound one of his ministers,' Lingard murmured softly, 'and I think he's about to join us.'

Gathercole entered the screen's containment of light, blinking in the glare, obviously hastily dressed and wearing a purple scarf in place of his dog-collar. He could see the hand in its grotesque exposure and he wasn't liking what he saw.

'Good morning, Mr Gathercole,' Rogers said with no desire now to be unfriendly. 'I'm afraid that the Church's authority appears to have been undermined by a hungry fox. I assume that you're now satisfied I wasn't imagining things?'

'I was in error, Mr Rogers, if that is what you wish me to say.' Repugnance was in his expression and he turned his head from the grave as though he had never seen a dead body before. He didn't seem curious enough to want to know how the police had discovered the exposed hand in the middle of the night and Rogers had no intention of volunteering it. 'Who is he?' he asked.

Burke and Hare had reached the body, uncovering a patch of dark blue cloth and the gilt button of a blazer. Rogers would have liked to have said that he certainly wasn't the late Mr Harland crawling early from his coffin for the last trump, but the clergyman's admission of error had disarmed him and he said instead, 'He was Richard Knostig of Nympton Manor. Was he a parishioner of yours?'

'No, no, he was not.' Gathercole shivered although the night was warm, looking sick. 'I've not heard the name before. I'd . . . had I better go now?'

'You're welcome to stay around, but it won't be pleasant,' Rogers said discouragingly, meaning that he'd rather he got himself out of the way. It wasn't the occasion for any non-productive theological discussion Gathercole might think appropriate.

'No, I'd rather not. Perhaps you'll excuse me and give me more information in the morning. I'll need to have the grave re-covered.' He turned and left the screened area and Rogers could hear him stumbling blindly in the outside darkness.

Lingard said, 'Very curious, George. The fella looked as though he'd done the deed himself, never even asked how chummy had died. He'd know more than anybody about the fresh grave, of course.'

'I'm glad he's not your grandmother, David. You'd have had him in handcuffs by now.'

'An idle thought,' Lingard was being flippant, 'before you latched on to him yourself and claimed all the credit.'

The body was wholly uncovered now and one of the P.C.s was brushing loose soil from Knostig's face with a painting brush Rogers had given him from his murder box. As definition emerged the photographer's electronic flash threw into sharp relief the planes of the sunken-in cheeks, the skin tinged with yellow. The teeth were bared in the black cavity of an open mouth; the eyes, depressed in their sockets, partly open and dulled with dirt. There was nothing to show the cause of his death and, whatever it was, he appeared not to have liked it. His expression suggested that he might have been calling for help from beneath his two feet of earth.

Rogers was at his most confident with insentient things – and they included dead bodies – which, while they might sometimes mislead, did so unwittingly. They did not lie, hold back on information or try to persuade him to believe that which he should not. Relieving Burke and Hare of their distasteful task – certain that neither would apply in the future for a CID appointment – he stooped and leaned over the most truthful witness of all, holding his breath and steeling his will against the revulsion of touching dead flesh. He unbuttoned the blazer and opened it out. There was nothing on the shirt to indicate a puncturing of the skin. Turning the body on to its side he examined the back. That, too, was free of bloodstaining, although he noticed patches of short yellow hairs or fibres on the seat of the trousers. Knostig had neither been shot nor stabbed to death nor, from the absence of symptoms in his features, strangled either. Easing the body back, he searched the pockets of the blazer and trousers. But for a crumpled piece of paper pushed to the bottom of the inner breast pocket and a handkerchief in the trousers, they were empty. No wallet, no house or car keys and no loose coins. He was certainly not taking anything with him.

Rogers grunted and straightened his legs, regarding the body with a satisfaction tempered with pity for the man who had gone from it. 'You'll have noticed that the spectacles are missing, David,' he said. 'And Lockersbie didn't mention them either. Oddly enough, neither did Mrs Knostig in her description of him. Dammit! I'd missed that.'

'A point,' Lingard conceded. 'And so had I. They either fell off before he was dumped in the porch or he wasn't wearing them when he died.'

'He had his photograph taken with them on, so he wore them habitually. Except, perhaps, in bed, having a bath or apparently while being unlawfully buried.' He decided he would worry about the nuances of dying myopically when he knew through which hole death had entered.

He had heard the racketing sounds of a car being pulled up at the entrance to the churchyard, recognizing its long-obsolescent engine as it faltered to silence. 'Bridget,' he said. 'Stand by for a wigging for being called out at night again.'

Even in the hard-edged illumination of floodlights at nearly four o'clock on a graveyard morning, Bridget Jane Hunter, Doctor of Medicine and Graduate in Morbid Pathology, was beautiful, her copper hair swinging around a face that showed none of the traumas of being called out of bed, her dark-orange eyes unpuffed by disturbed sleep. She wore lithely a smooth oatmeal-coloured suit and carried a black bag of what Rogers called her butchery tools.

She was the reason for Rogers's wife leaving him, an on-and-off liaison he had yet to stabilize and was not too certain that he wished to. It was made frustrating by police regulations, inhibited as much by medical ethics and his own built-in puritanical guilt. And he mistrusted the occasional fierceness of her need for him, suspecting that it might be only one facet of a promiscuity in which he would want no part. He was a man difficult to convince that he might be the only one. They were two bodies well-matched in sensuality, each needing the other's physical chemistry, but with personas which didn't fit too often or too comfortably. It didn't make for an easy working rela-tionship either, for now, in one of their periodic troughs, they were each waiting for the other to concede a minor sort of defeat which would signify an ending they both needed to the held-back release of their sexual appetites. A need, Rogers reminded himself occasionally in his bleaker moments, only a degree or two less painful than banging one's head against a wooden post.

'I'm sorry, Bridget,' he said to her with exaggerated contri-tion, 'but I really do try and get my bodies unearthed during office hours.'

'It's quite all right.' She was impersonal, her attention on the body in the opened grave. 'I wasn't doing anything but sleep-ing.'

He smiled, lowering his voice. 'But nice to see you again. It's been too long.'

55

'Only from one murder to another,' she said ironically and there was no return smile. 'I assume that this is one?'

'It must be, but I don't know how.' He gave her the details of what he did know and they were few enough.

She laid her bag on the grass and crouched at the side of the body, scrutinizing the features, then opening wider the eyelids with her thumb. Rogers, standing over her, could smell above the odour of the dead man the hyacinth scent she wore. Perhaps, he thought against the odds, she had put it on for him.

'It's difficult in this light,' she said, 'and with so much soil in them, but the pupils appear to be excessively dilated.'

'Significant of what, Bridget?' He could make a couple of guesses, both probably wrong, and she would, in her present mood, chop him down if he made them.

'Significant of nothing at the moment, and I'm sure you don't want a lecture on the muscular fibres of the eyes. I have to consider other factors and that won't happen here.' She flexed one of the dead arms and then a leg. 'You wish to know how long?'

'It's of the utmost.' He did a mental calculation. 'He's been missing about two-and-a-half days – say 56 hours – and he was seen dead by Lockersbie about 27 hours ago. Does that help?'

'Not much,' she said shortly. 'Rigor mortis has passed off and that would be accelerated by the high temperatures. There's an onset of putrefaction – again helped by the temperature . . .' She frowned as she thought. 'Don't hold me to it, but I'd say somewhere around the 40-hour mark.'

'But you'll narrow it down when you have him on the table.' It wasn't a question, for he knew she would.

'Yes.' She wasn't really with him, but thinking things out. 'And don't ask me yet how he died because I don't know and can't guess. I can only assure you that he is dead.'

'I'd like to know soon, Bridget.' His affability with the world was being abraded.

'I'm certain you would, but it's not possible. I have an important meeting at nine o'clock. If you get him to the mortuary immediately, I'll do a quick external examination and check as much as I can on the time of death. I won't need you there and I'll telephone through with what information I have.' She stood and picked up her bag. 'I shall be free to do the complete examination about noon.'

She hadn't once called him George or given him the grave regard of her eyes, but looked at him as though he were unlikeable. It underlined the coolness she must feel for him and it produced in him an unwanted irritation with her. 'He'll be down there in less than fifteen minutes,' he said tersely and saying it to her back as she left him.

Lingard was taking snuff with an elaborate disinterest and he followed Rogers out from the screens. The chill in the air had not escaped his notice, but one of the things he had learned in his 29 years was when to keep his mouth cautiously shut.

Rogers was scowling and muttering, 'Damn and bloody damn!' and that did not invite comment either.

10

Rogers and Lingard sat in an otherwise deserted Senior Officers' Mess and ate grilled gammon rashers and fried eggs sent in from the canteen. With the smell of the dead Knostig still clinging to the cilia in his nostrils, Rogers was not so hungry for breakfast as he had anticipated. He picked diffidently at it while Lingard ate with what he thought an indecent enjoyment.

'You know, David,' he said, 'if we can accept Bridget's estimate that Knostig died not too long after he left home, then when Lockersbie saw him in the porch his body had been sculling around in parts unknown for about twenty hours. And that takes in all day Thursday.'

'Waiting for darkness, of course.' Lingard knew that Rogers

was using him as a sounding-board for his speculating. 'Dark deeds need it.'

'Yes. And knowing about that grave. It bothers me. Check back on the *Post and Messenger* and see if there's a report on Harland's burial.' He laid his knife and fork on the plate of his unfinished breakfast, killing its taste with a drink of coffee. 'They must have fried that in multigrade engine oil,' he complained perversely. 'Where was I? Ah, yes. There has to be a connection. You don't take a body into a churchyard in the hope that there's a conveniently freshly-dug grave. And why leave it in the porch? Was he – or she – disturbed by Lockersbie?'

'I'd buy that. Why not? Whoever it was must have been keeping quiet to see what he'd do. And I'm sure he'd have been recognized as a drunk looking for a place to kip down. When he'd gone there'd still be no option but to go on with the burying.'

'He could have been going to report it to the police. Which he did eventually. It'd be taking a hell of a chance.'

'Were it me, I'd have followed him to see what he did. Seeing him collapse in the car park would have given me the go-ahead.'

'A possibility.' Rogers didn't sound too convinced. 'But he must have palsied with fear whoever was doing it.'

'Or them,' Lingard said. 'A mite difficult for one person to hump an adult body around.'

'Agreed. But not impossible. Nor unlikely. All that would be simple of explanation,' he added sardonically, 'if we knew who wanted him dead.'

'If you won't accept the saintly Gathercole, what about Mrs Knostig? She's a hefty woman and you said she doesn't like him. I always put my money on embittered females.'

'If all unloving wives went that far, we married men would soon be an endangered species. Women have much more subtle ways than murder for getting rid of unwanted husbands. For the moment I'll stick with the old formula that sex or greed plus its frustrations add up to a need to do something nasty in proportion to the pressure it exerts. Of course,' he said, scowling, 'with Bridget being so bloody-minded, we still don't know how he died. Just to make my day, it wouldn't surprise me to be told that he'd died of a double hernia or measles. That's what's so bloody irritating. Nobody but us seems to be particularly worried about the poor bugger, least of all his wife. Or the Blandford girl if it comes to that. And I don't suppose the gardener gives a damn either.'

'What about Miss Blandford, George?' Lingard asked. 'Might she not have something to do with Knostig's unpopularity? You seemed a mite enthusiastic about her delectability.'

'True, although she's not the sort to give me hot flushes,' he lied phlegmatically. 'I've been innoculated against it by marriage. But I'd guess that she'd be a disturbing influence wherever she was. Against there being a discovered adultery, she and Mrs Knostig were acting quite matey. No tension while I was with them, no frozen looks. Which reminds me. After you've finished stuffing your face with breakfast, dig out the manager of the Beaux Arts and find out where the actor chap Humfries with an "f" lives. Then go and have words with him. When I've changed my shirt I'll be breaking what might be deliriously happy news to Mrs Knostig. And before I forget it.' He pulled out his wallet and handed Lingard the piece of paper he had found in Knostig's pocket. 'What do you make of that, David?'

Lingard read the numbers on it: *1620793, 1620110, 1620131, 4260261*. 'Telephone numbers,' he said, 'the first three local.' He shook his head. 'The other means nothing to me.'

'Reverse it, David.' Rogers was smiling.

'I see what you mean. Damn!' It was obvious and he should have seen it. 'Another local one. I didn't anticipate your formidable intellect, George.'

'I imagine it was meant to fob off a wife's curiosity. Which makes it significant. Check all four, David, and see what they give us.'

A P.C. opened the door, looked cautiously in and then

approached their table. Handing Rogers a message form, he said, 'Sorry it's a bit delayed, sir. We tried everywhere but couldn't locate you before.'

Rogers said 'Thank you,' unable to quarrel with the implication made that the Mess was an unlikely place to find a couple of investigating officers at six-thirty in the morning, and waited until the P.C. had gone before reading it.

To: D/Supt. G. Rogers, HQ/CID.
From: Dr B. J. Hunter, Pathology Department.
Time/date: 5.50 a.m. 19th August.
Subject: Richard Knostig (deceased).
Preliminary examination and findings. Estimated elapse of 45-50 hours from death. No external symptoms of cause. Contact pressure marks on thighs, abdomen and chest. Hypostasis advanced anterior trunk. Full examination arranged 12.30 p.m.

He grunted and passed it to Lingard. 'Bridget at her least helpful, David. He apparently died on his belly or, at least, was left lying on it for several hours. Which should tell us something if I could think what it was.'

Lingard, having read it, returned the form. 'Only that it's the done thing to die of natural causes on your back and that we needn't worry too much about chummy dying of a double hernia or whatever.'

'I was trying to be witty,' Rogers said heavily, too early in the morning for him to bear misunderstanding with equanimity. 'Somehow I can't make myself think up a good reason for secretly burying anyone who hadn't first been murdered.'

I I

If there was a conventional time and manner of breaking the news of a man's death to his wife, Rogers had never heard of it. It was an unwanted chore he had done often enough, suspecting on occasions that he suffered more than the recipient of his bad news. He had been wept on, but he had also been cursed obscenely, called a heartless liar and been engaged in non-stop conversations about everything but the fact of the dead person. He thought that he knew why, but in particular it had added to his fogginess in ever understanding women.

Having showered and changed his clothing, which he imagined reeked of Knostig's corruption, and doused his body with a deodorant to guard against its lingering, he had returned to his office to wait for nine o'clock, judging it a reasonable enough time to call on an unknowing widow. Part of his waiting had been employed in preparing a Crime Release for the news-hawks already badgering the official Press Liaison Officer and in refusing interviews to local radio and a television crew. Personal publicity was something he could always do without and, if in nothing else, in that he believed himself a rarity in the police service.

On his desk were the print-outs of the routine name checks he had had made on the Information Room computer. Against the names Olivia Knostig, Helen Blandford and Martin Humfries there was nothing. Richard Francis Knostig had recorded against him six years earlier a conviction for driving with an undue proportion of alcohol in the blood, having been fined £200 and disqualified from driving for twelve months. Arthur Wimbush had been placed on probation and fined twenty-one years ago for stealing ferrets and for the larceny of cigarettes and cigars valued at £6.12s.11d. from a tobacco kiosk; thereafter, an uncommitted or undetected nothing. 'Big stuff,' Rogers muttered to himself. It wasn't exactly top-league villainy, only the small change of the checking of a man's antecedents.

He saw Wimbush in one of the netted structures when he entered the drive of Nympton Manor and accepted that if he ran true to form he would be neither friendly nor particularly helpful when interviewed, but easier on that account to deal with.

Helen Blandford opened the door to his knocking and he saw

again the shadow of unease in her eyes. She looked, he thought, more attractive each time he saw her. It was not an occasion for smiling and he didn't. 'I'd like to speak to Mrs Knostig,' he said, 'and I think that you'd better be with her when I do.'

She stared at him wordlessly as though a sort of doom was written in his expression, then led him along the passage, where the disorder and dust were apparently permanent. She left him and entered the laboratory, reappearing after what he thought an unduly long murmuring of muffled talk from inside. 'Mrs Knostig will see you,' she said, which sounded condescending and irritated him.

Mrs Knostig, seated at the binocular microscope, looked up at him over the brass eyepieces, set-faced and without greeting. Then she stood, obviously not allowing herself to remain at an inferior level to a standing man. She wore the same shirt and skirt as she had the day before, her hair strained rigidly back from her forehead. Rogers thought that she had a feminine intuition of trouble, for there was apprehension in her eyes.

'I'm sorry, Mrs Knostig,' he said, 'but it's very bad news, I'm afraid. Your husband is dead.' It was brutal, he supposed, but what other way was there that did anything but prolong the suffering? It was like death itself; better that it were sudden than drawn out.

The flesh of her face tightened and she lifted her chin, her fingers plucking at her skirt. There was the counterpoint of a small gasp from the girl behind him, but no Oh, my God!, moist eyes or stricken bewilderment from Mrs Knostig, and he hadn't expected it. Then, as though to show that he had misjudged her, she turned her back to him to face the illuminated gazebo of buffeting moths, clenching her fists and hunching her shoulders. Helen Blandford went to her, putting an arm protectively around her and making comforting noises. She, he noticed, was taking the news more stoically although her face might be a shade or two paler beneath the tan. Between them, their attitudes made him feel as though he had threatened them with violence.

While he waited, the non-existent man in the room, his eyes took in the detail of the laboratory, an habitual storing of impressions, mental photographs for later developing and a faculty made sharp-edged by years of necessary observation of the apparently irrelevant. The small cages took up most of the work-bench space. They all contained vegetation. In some of them he recognized the foliage of potato. Others had bunches of unidentifiable leaves, a few with either white, scarlet or purple berries. The caterpillars crawling and writhing over them ranged in size from orange-yellow dwarves with black heads to six-inch yellow monsters with violet stripes and a curved horn on the tail. There were setting boards on one of the benches, each with columns of identical moths with wings outstretched and pinned nose-to-tail; clear plastic boxes each with two moths captive inside, and jars of white crystals. The moths in the brightly-lit gazebo, blundering clumsily against the glass or resting on the lush growths of plants, were mainly heavy-bodied, brown and yellow, with a small patch of dirty white on their drab backs. With them, slender and quicker in flight, were numbers of smaller crimson and black moths. The narrow-drawered mahogany cabinets fitted between the benches must, Rogers considered, contain the pinned specimens which seemed so expendable in the name of scientific research.

'It's quite all right, dear,' the older woman said, turning back to face the detective. She was dry-eyed but, he thought, bracing herself for further blows. 'You've found him?' she asked.

That was obvious, having told her that he was dead. 'Yes,' he said, 'but there's more. I've very good reasons for believing that he was murdered.'

This time her reaction was of shocked surprise, her mouth shaking, grey eyes riveted on him with incredulity. 'No!' she cried, 'you're mistaken. That can't be and I don't believe it. You don't know what you're saying.'

Christ, he swore in his mind, *Please don't be too bloody difficult.* To her, he said, 'He was found this morning buried in the Saint

Boniface churchyard, Mrs Knostig. In another man's grave. It's a reasonable assumption that he was killed by whoever buried him.'

'It isn't possible.' She shook her head, denying it with a return of her arrogance. She moved away from him as though she found his proximity unpleasant. 'Will you leave me for a few minutes. I wish to compose myself.' To Helen Blandford she said, 'Please stay. The superintendent knows where the sitting-room is.' Then again to him, crisply and appearing composed enough already, speaking as though he might touch a forelock and shuffle away. 'Help yourself to a drink if you wish. I won't keep you long.'

He sat in there, chewing on the stem of his empty pipe, having refused himself the offered drink and pondering on the bossiness of her type of woman, wondering what feelings of insecurity it might be used to conceal and whether very small bosoms were indicative of it. Despite what he took to be her agitation, he had sensed nothing of black sorrow for her dead husband, only shock at the realization of his death. Behind that, he couldn't believe that she gave a damn, and he felt that he wasn't being too unkind in thinking her a fit mate for a rhinoceros. That there was an underlying antagonism towards him he accepted as being directed at his function as a policeman and the bearer of bad news. When Helen Blandford came for him he had decided that he need not fear his questions would land him with an hysterical and weeping woman.

Mrs Knostig, standing at an open window, turned as he entered, no more friendly for his short absence. With no preamble she said, 'How did he die?'

'I don't know, but I will later this morning.'

'Do you know who did it?'

'Not yet.'

'But you'll find out.'

'Given enough information from those who were close to him,' he said pointedly, 'I probably will. Which means that despite the shock this must be to you, I shall have to ask you a few questions. Do you mind? I want you to be quite certain that you wish it.'

'I don't wish it, but if you have to ask them do so.'

'On your own, Mrs Knostig. I need to speak to Miss Blandford separately.'

She frowned. 'Oh! Why?'

'There will have to be an inquest and it's necessary to avoid any unconscious influences when interviewing potential witnesses,' he explained, anticipating she would resent it anyway.

If she did, it didn't show. 'Would you mind, Helen?' she said.

'I'll see you afterwards,' Rogers said to her.

She looked at Mrs Knostig as though for approval and then back at him. 'Of course,' she agreed, 'I shall be in the sitting-room.'

When the door closed behind her, Mrs Knostig moved to a chair at the desk and sat, upright and straight-backed. Rogers, uninvited but unwilling to remain standing, planted himself on a space on a work-bench. It didn't appear to meet with her approval, but he tried to look pleasant, showing at the same time a proper sympathy for her widowhood and finding it difficult.

'First of all,' he said, 'your husband was found without his spectacles. He would have gone out wearing them?'

It wasn't apparently what she expected and for a moment she hesitated. 'Yes, most certainly. It was necessary that he should.'

'His wallet, keys and so on were also missing.'

'Is that why you think he was killed? That he was robbed?' She could have been referring to a stranger for all the emotion she showed.

'I wouldn't think so, but you should advise his bank about the cheque book and credit cards.'

She nodded, but said nothing.

'When he went out on Wednesday afternoon, was there anything said or done to suggest where he was going? You said that there'd been an argument.'

65

'And I told you I was not prepared to discuss it. I didn't ask him where he was going and he didn't tell me. He lived his own life and I wasn't curious enough to want to know.'

'Was that because of the estrangement between you? Because you occupy separate bedrooms?' Bull-at-a-gate Rogers, he thought, asking to be shouted at.

She remained calm, not demanding how he had known. 'My husband and I were not on good terms. I told you that yesterday.'

'Was there another woman?' A murdered man must, he assured himself, be some sort of an excuse for bluntness.

Her face mottled pink; not, he guessed, from embarrassment. 'That's a question in bad taste, superintendent.'

'Yes,' he said, 'it probably is, but the fact of his murder makes it a necessary one. Was there?' he asked again.

'No, there was not,' she said with emphasis. 'I would have known had there been.'

That could be true, Rogers knew from unhappy experience, most wives possessing a dismaying intuition where their husband's affections were concerned. 'You told me that he drank and was quarrelsome because of it. I know he had been convicted of drunken driving, so was he a heavy drinker?'

'Yes, he was. It was the cause of our – as you put it – estrangement.'

'Did he resent it?'

'If he didn't, I did.'

'You refused to tell me about his friends and associates, Mrs Knostig. Will you tell me now?'

'He had no friends,' she said flatly. 'Heavy drinkers rarely do. Miss Blandford gave you the name of one of his acquaintances. Whatever others he had were connected with his business and do not live locally.'

'He drank alone?'

'Yes, so far as I knew.'

'So he presumably had problems?'

'Not necessarily. If he had, I didn't know of them.'

'Mrs Knostig.' He was coming to the bit where she would inevitably bristle nastily at the least or explode at the most. 'An understandable reaction to being questioned about one's movements by the police is to believe that you are suspected of something. That isn't necessarily so. We are trying to find out facts we can work on. We start in ignorance, aren't able to read minds, and guesswork is no help in finding out a murdered man's last movements.'

He waited but she said nothing, holding his gaze with expressionless eyes. The fingers and thumb of one of her hands were being rubbed against each other with a soft slithering noise. He thought it a sign either of nervousness or irritated impatience.

'Your husband probably died during the evening or night following his leaving here. For my records, to help me, I'd like to know where you were during that time.'

There was a taut silence, her face darkening. Then she said in a voice trembling with anger, 'How dare you! How dare you ask me that! You . . . you are questioning where I was! Do you think . . .' She choked on her words, glaring at him.

'I'm not thinking anything at the moment, Mrs Knostig,' he said patiently, unruffled by her outburst. 'It's a question I propose asking everybody I interview. It could be relevant and I did explain why.'

She was stiff now, only her eyes hostile. 'I don't like your attitude, superintendent.'

'No,' he agreed, 'it isn't much, is it? Where were you, please?'

'Damn you, I was here. All afternoon, all evening and all night. If you doubt my word, as you appear about to, you will be speaking to Miss Blandford. She was here with me.'

'And the following night?'

'That also.'

He slid from the work-bench and stood, his buttocks numb from the hard surface. 'May I see his bedroom, Mrs Knostig? There might be something there I . . .'

She cut his words short, standing and angry again. 'No, you

may not. There is nothing there that could possibly interest you.' Her voice rose with her indignation. 'I am sure your warrant to investigate my husband's death does not include searching his house and subjecting his wife to impertinent questions.' She stared at him as though she couldn't believe it possible. 'You even think that I might have something to do with my husband's death!'

He held her eyes for a long time until the anger had gone from them. 'I'm sorry I've upset you,' he said formally, 'and I've only one more matter. It's necessary that your husband's body is identified. Will you do that?'

'No.' She turned her head from him, but not before he had seen the flinching from its prospect in her face. 'There must be somebody else. Now please go, I wish to be left alone.'

Walking back along the passage to the sitting-room, he supposed it was one thing to kill and dismember butterflies and moths and quite another to look at the face of a dead husband. There had been another woman, of that he was certain, even though he couldn't put a finger on why he should be. Apart from the fact that she had almost certainly lied to him, he had learned something from the interview. And not only that as well as not liking her husband, the formidable Mrs Knostig was not exactly infatuated with Detective Superintendent Rogers either. Which now made two of them; she and Bridget.

12

As well as a passion for Regency waistcoats and silk shirts, Lingard had an emotional relationship with his cherished Bentley, a glossy green monster of veteran vintage with stainless steel exhaust pipes sprouting from her long strapped-down bonnet. He loved her and, as when he had fallen in love with the now dead Nancy Frail, it brought with it the same anguishes and anxieties. He drove and parked her with dark foreboding that some clumsy oaf would collide with her, crumpling an irreplaceable mudguard or scratching the flawless paintwork. He nightmared in his sleep that she had been stolen and, awake, would no more allow another man to drive her than, were he married, to allow him to sleep with his wife.

With the canvas hood folded back and his shaggy blond hair bared to the warm airflow, he manoeuvred her with exaggerated caution through early morning streets already packed with jockeying traffic for what he hoped were informative words from Martin Humfries. The Theatre Director of the Beaux Arts, not apparently overly affectionate towards Humfries, had told him that when last heard from he was lodging with a Mrs Cunninghame in Bullers Road, that he had been employed in a minor part in a play and at the end of its scheduled run a month earlier had been rested. A euphemism, Lingard guessed, for being given the boot. And, indeed, on being pressed the Director had said that Humfries would not take direction and therefore would not be offered another part. Other than that, he had been stubborn in refusing to discuss him further.

Lingard found a parking space in Bullers Road, satisfying himself that it was an unlikely milieu for car thieves or reckless drivers. The houses looked pleasantly non-modern in the sun, decaying with a middle-class dignity and haunted, he was sure, by the gentle rattle of afternoon cups of tea. He climbed the steps of No. 35 – it was also called *Blenheim* – into a porch of pots of scarlet geraniums recently watered and pressed the bell-push at the side of the immaculate white-painted door.

The woman opening it was elderly, faded, smelled faintly of perfumed talc and was as immaculate as her door. If Lingard ever wanted an extra grandmother she would be somebody like her.

'Mrs Cunninghame?' he asked with a smile he reserved for nice old ladies. 'I'm sorry to bother you, but is Mr Humfries at home?'

She smiled back at him. 'He's in his room. Please come in and I'll call him.'

He stood in the hall while she climbed the stairs, then heard her knocking on a door.

The man who came down was stocky and athletic and manifestly a cheerful extrovert, ready to be friendly with anyone and totally unlike Lingard's preconception of an actor. He wore narrow and tight blue trousers with a lemon-yellow open-neck shirt and a cravat. His damp sandy hair and scrubbed freshness indicated that he was not too long out of a bath. 'Hello,' he said affably when he reached the detective, 'and what can I do for you?'

Lingard fished in a pocket for his warrant card. 'I'm a police officer,' he said, 'and I . . .'

The effect on Humfries was cataclysmic. His smile vanished, his mouth opened and there was stricken panic in his eyes. A moaning sound came from him and he twisted convulsively, running wildly along the hall and through a door at its end into a kitchen, leaving the astonished Lingard still holding out the warrant card.

His reaction to the sudden flight was slowed for a moment by his being in another's house, by Mrs Cunninghame standing at the top of the stairs and watching him in bewilderment. Calling out 'Excuse me!' he took off after the vanished Humfries, reaching the open door simultaneously with the arrival beneath his feet of a dachshund dog.

Swerving to avoid tripping over it, his shoulder hit the doorpost and he fell heavily with an impact that shuddered anguish into his skull and drove the breath from his lungs. He lay there dazed, deflated by the manner in which Humfries' flight had taken him by surprise, angry at him and at his own inelegant floundering, but glad that he hadn't fallen on the very small dog which had now also disappeared.

When he believed he could breathe again he stood and staggered to the doorway leading to the rear garden. An empty greenhouse and a lawn surrounded by flower borders offered no conccalmcnt. A gate in the panel fencing at its end was open and it needed no more for him to accept defeat. Taking snuff in a nose that felt flattened and flicking cautiously away the loose grains with his red silk handkerchief, he returned to the hall. The old lady was there with the tan-coloured dog in her arms. Both were trembling and she looked frightened.

'I'm sorry about that, Mrs Cunninghame,' he said gently, combing his hair straight with his fingers. 'I'm a police officer and you needn't be alarmed. 'I don't know why he should run like that.' He showed her his warrant card. 'That's all I did, and you're not proposing to run away, are you?'

She smiled nervously but apparently reassured, for he was in his patrician foppishness as unlike a granny-basher as a man could be. 'No, of course not. Has he done something? He's such a nice boy.'

'He must have done, but I wouldn't know what. I was only here to ask him a few questions about a friend of his.'

'I'm sure it can't be very serious.' She appeared anxious to minimize whatever villainy her lodger had committed, as Lingard knew a nice old lady would.

'Probably not, but I'd like to look in his room.' He smiled, making it a small matter.

'Oh, dear, don't you need a warrant or something?' she asked doubtfully.

'Not if you personally have no objection, and I'm sure that you haven't. He *is* a lodger, isn't he?'

'A paying guest,' she corrected him, for she still had her pride. 'And I don't mind if it's the right thing to do.'

'You come with me, Mrs Cunninghame, and see fair play,' he said, crouching and patting the dachshund she had put down. It had lost him a likely prisoner but he held no hard feelings.

She led him upstairs and into Humfries' room, standing in the doorway while he searched it and clearly worried at what he was doing. He thought that Humfries had been a well-looked-after man to occupy a bed-sitter such as this. It was all pink-rose patterned cretonne and glossy pre-war walnut with a bed big enough to accommodate a polygamist's responsibilities, all spotlessly clean and filled with sunshine.

The wardrobe and drawers were short on clothing and Humfries' personal effects minimal. In a drawer, Lingard found an Unemployment Benefit Attendance card in the name of H. Pritt and a calfskin wallet containing £75 in £10 and £5 notes, two coloured snapshots of an extraordinarily attractive girl, an expired driver's licence and a cheque card, both also issued to H. Pritt. In another drawer, tucked between the folds of a laundered shirt, were three torn-out Lloyds Bank cheques with *Richard Francis Knostig* printed on them and two empty envelopes from a London theatrical agent addressed to Martin Humfries Esq., care of a guest house in Thorpe Bay. Apart from a few unconcealed news-clippings of reviews of plays in which Humfries had been mentioned and an album of stage photographs, all including Humfries, the other impedimenta supporting the life-style of a lodger could have belonged to anybody.

It was of no comfort to Lingard to know why Humfries had fled so precipitously. The fear of being found in possession of cheques stolen from a dead man would lend wings to the feet of any but the most nerveless of villians. But it left him with the feeling of a man who had hit an unexpected jackpot and received an outpouring of unspendable money. Returning downstairs with Mrs Cunninghame to question her further about her absconded lodger did nothing to help him in accepting philosophically his escape, or his having to explain it satisfactorily to Rogers.

13

When Rogers knocked on the panel of the door and entered, Helen Blandford was sitting curled in a chair smoking a cigarette. Her eyes, dark and liquid in the sunshine streaming through the windows, regarded him with what he thought was calculating wariness. Her white dress gave her skin a deeper coppery tinge, clinging loosely to a body that, despite it, remained tiny and fragile. As, he guessed, she had intended; making him feel large, coarse and aggressively masculine. It also irritated him because his only too likely speculation about the colour of the skin beneath the dress would remind him of his fallibility, prove again that he had human failings and clog his thinking with unwanted lechery.

He sat opposite her in a chair out of the sunlight, took out his notebook and pen and said with a wry grin, 'The mole's returned to dig out more worms.' With her, a woman who had tried to use her sexual attractiveness on him, he was going to have less reason to avoid scratching at sensibilities. And, having grown used to being treated as a leper by non-smokers, he looked at her cigarette with approval. 'Do you mind my smoking?' he asked.

'No,' she said. 'Please do.' There was a shadow of apprehension in her eyes as she looked at the open notebook on his lap.

Looking at her and not at what he was doing, not speaking but allowing the waiting silence to grow, he filled his pipe and lit it, blowing the smoke through the window at his side. When one of them had to say something, he asked casually, 'Did you like Mr Knostig?'

Whatever she had expected, it hadn't been that. Her eyebrows lifted and she stiffened.

'It's a time for frankness,' he said, not so casually. 'He was murdered and I have a duty to find out by whom. That demands nothing less than unvarnished facts.' Despite his warning, he knew he would be foolish to expect them, not to be lied to.

She bit at her lower lip. 'I didn't like him,' she said flatly.

'Why?'

'How many reasons do you want?'

'All of them.' He wished to God that she would pull her dress down below her knees.

'He drank too much, was a groper and wore dirty shirts.'

Sounding fairly normal, Rogers thought cynically, but glad that he had put on a fresh shirt. 'He pawed you?' he asked, wanting to know if that were all.

'He tried to. And tried hard at getting into my bed,' she said laconically. 'Too often to be amusing. On two occasions he even followed me to Kirk's Pipe.'

He raised his eyebrows at that. Kirk's Pipe lay high on the moor, a rock-strewn wilderness riddled with dangerous vertical caves into which sheep occasionally fell to their deaths.

'I go there to collect cinnabars and when I wish to get away from people,' she said in answer to his unspoken question.

'Persistence is the hall-mark of a successful lover, Miss Blandford.'

'Really?' she said disdainfully. 'I wouldn't know, but I assure you that he wasn't successful. Now you know why we didn't want him back.'

'Mrs Knostig knew then?'

'Of course. He wasn't the most subtle of men.'

'But that wasn't the cause of the quarrel she had with him before he left.' He was fishing positively.

She hesitated, looking at him speculatively, plainly wondering whether he already knew. 'No,' she said.

'No,' he agreed as though he did know. 'So what was it?'

'He had been insisting on the necessity of selling the house and Mrs Knostig didn't wish him to. He was actually seeing the estate agents that afternoon.'

74

'And who are they?'

'I don't know.'

'All of which is something Mrs Knostig was too embarrassed to tell me.' He tried hard to keep irony from his words.

'It isn't anything you should expect to be told by her,' she retorted sharply. 'He wished to do it and she didn't. Her . . . our work would be ruined were we to move.'

'Why did he have to sell it?'

'I am trying to help, Mr Rogers, and I hope that I am not being disloyal.' She took a deep breath. 'His finances were desperately shaky. He had commitments he couldn't meet, had no prospects of meeting. That alone couldn't seriously affect us because Mrs Knostig's work is financed by a university grant. But moving to heaven knows where, reorganizing the laboratory, the breeding and plant cages would.' She shook her head irritably. 'He got himself into a mess and us with it.'

'What are the details of the mess?' She had been moving restlessly in the chair, causing her dress to rise above her tucked-under legs. Only an inch or so higher, but tending to be mesmeric to the detective even though he kept his eyes on hers. He wondered with the idle part of his mind what perversity made a thigh, looked at without prurience on a beach, so erotic when meant to be concealed under a dress.

'I honestly don't know for sure,' she said, 'but after the butterfly farm folded he obviously had an insufficient income. I believe he owed a lot to the Inland Revenue. Does it matter?'

'Not to him now, that's for certain. But it does to me. He was supposed to have had £80 in his wallet. That's quite a bit of spending money for a man who's supposed to be broke.'

She shrugged. 'I don't think that's anything. He wouldn't have thought it much, either. He was broke for big amounts, not drinking money.'

'We do live in different worlds,' Rogers murmured, although he couldn't fit it in with a run-down house and a decaying car. 'The gardener wouldn't come for nothing.'

'He's paid mostly out of the research grant.' A *Why would you want to know that?* showed in her expression, but wasn't uttered.

'Perhaps you'll tell me, Miss Blandford,' he said, choosing his words carefully and as engagingly as he could. 'Knostig appears to have been a fairly warm-blooded man who was frustrated here in his home. There does have to be another woman somewhere, doesn't there?'

'Possibly there is. I wouldn't know or be interested. It's hardly anything he would have talked about.'

'But other people would.' When she remained silent, he said, 'I did mention there'll be an inquest. The coroner's a man who can ask some pretty searching questions of everybody called to give evidence at it. And he works from a police report.' He smiled to make it an irrelevant but routine necessity. 'Such as where were you on the night of the 16th August, sort of thing. For *my* report, that night and the one following. You aren't singled out,' he added. 'I ask it of everybody concerned.'

She was frowning, scratching inelegantly at her thigh and diverting some of his attention; he hoped for his peace of mind, unwittingly. 'I was here,' she said, not objecting as Mrs Knostig had. 'Either working or in bed.'

'Sitting up watching your caterpillars eating one another?'

She managed a brief smile at that. '*And* their imagos making nocturnal love.'

'That must be entertaining,' he said. 'It keeps you up late?'

'Sometimes. It happens that on the nights you mention it did not. But if you wish to know what time I went to bed, I can't remember.' There was a touch of mockery in her words. 'Mrs Knostig might, she does all the locking-up.'

'I'm quite happy,' he said blandly. 'It *is* only a formality. Did you ever know a Mr Harland? Ever hear his name mentioned?'

She creased her forehead and, watching her eyes, he was satisfied she had not. 'No. Is he another of your worms?'

'That's fairly apt, Miss Blandford. He's the man in whose grave Knostig was buried.'

She had shuddered then. 'That was a quite horrible thing to ask me.'

'Yes, it was,' he conceded. Agreeing nearly always left dispraisement with nothing to add to it. 'But as you've never heard of him . . .' He levered himself from his chair and replaced the notebook he hadn't used in his pocket. 'I think that's about all and I'm grateful for your help. I'm going to speak to your gardener chap now. On my way out and I won't take up too much of his time.'

She stood too and, were it not his ego deceiving him, he could read female interest in her dark eyes, sense a relaxing in her and, his questioning over, a ghost of rapport between them. Her scent reached out at him, stirring his sexual imagery while he cursed in his mind the restraints of his professional morality. Few women had done this to him and when they did he suffered.

'Will I . . will you be wanting to see me again?' she asked.

'Almost certainly,' he said, smiling down at her, insuring against future possibilities and noticing that her hair was perfumed also. 'And we don't have to fight all the time, do we?'

'You're definitely not anyone I wish to be unfriendly with,' she said, her lustrous eyes wide open. 'Do you ever stop being a policeman?'

He was certain – almost certain – that her eyes were saying *I approve of you and I'm waiting for you to do something about it*, and he liked forthright women. 'Only when I'm in my bath,' he said.

'I can't offer you a bath, but please don't go yet.'

He had to accept either that he was irresistibly yummy or that she still wanted to buy something from him. He regretted that it had to be the latter, and wondered where she had intended taking him with Mrs Knostig in the house. Whatever her motive, he wasn't prepared to wound her pride.

'I have to,' he said with a show of regret, looking at his wristwatch. 'I've an appointment at my office in half-an-hour. Otherwise . . .' He shrugged, looking without having to try hard a man frustrated by his work commitments.

Her eyes were evaluating his sincerity. 'Perhaps some other time,' she said lightly as if it didn't matter too much.

She saw him to the outside door and when her brown body brushed against his in the hall – he felt it was like being stroked with warm fur – he couldn't make up his mind whether it was accidental or not.

Now that it was too late, he knew he hadn't asked her all the questions he had intended, that he had allowed her femininity to blunt the edge of his probing. He also knew that before he saw her again he would have to do something to anaesthetize himself sexually, before his fallibility was proven by the sensuality that so disturbed his satyrish other self. And the outcome of that, depending on the state of the juices of his body, could be either the most sublime of activities or the most squalid. Not for the first time he wished – not too seriously – that he had been neutered as a pup.

14

Rogers, conscious of Helen Blandford watching him from the window, found Wimbush in one of the netted cages. In contrast to the neglected gardens it was meticulously neat, the soil raked and weed-free, a spade and fork standing in it clean and shiny. The plants in parade-ground rows were what he would expect to see in hedgerows and to which he would be unable to give names. Even with the entrance flap open it was stifling inside, the fine-meshed netting holding out against logic any cooling air.

Wimbush, cutting with secateurs at a bush, was aware of Rogers entering behind him, but did not look around. There was a studied insolence in his ignoring him that put him on the other side of Rogers's fence as a police-despising villain.

'I'm a detective officer,' he said politely enough, 'and I'd like a few words with you.'

'Yer,' he answered without turning his head from what he

was doing. 'I know 'oo you are.'

Rogers waited a few moments, then snapped, 'I'm not here because I've nothing else to do, so give me your attention. I don't intend speaking to the back of your neck.'

Wimbush straightened himself and turned slowly to a stern Rogers, his face a dull red and breathing heavily. 'I got things to finish, mate,' he growled.

'So have I,' Rogers said tersely. It wasn't a good start for digging out information. 'A damned sight more important than what you're doing.'

Because he was a man Rogers would want to remember anyway, he photographed him visually, storing the impressions in his mind. Small pig's eyes that showed distaste for the detective in a meaty, sweaty face pock-marked like the moon's surface and with the indefinable reflection of a cunning mind showing on it. A grease-stained check cap pulled down to his eyebrows and green overalls stretched taut over a shirtless brawny body and arms, ending at the sleeves with hands like bristled cured hams. A rough physical male with the smell of beer on his breath and the sourness of sweat on his body. A man against whom, if words became heated, Rogers would need to have a clenched fist ready. Hard enough himself, he still wouldn't like to quarrel with him over a couple of ferrets and a few cigarettes. He discarded the rhinoceros as a mate for Mrs Knostig, substituting the more compatible policeman-hating Wimbush.

They stared at each other for long seconds with Rogers bearing down on him with the stronger will before Wimbush said, 'All right, mate, no offence. What d'you want?'

'I'm making enquiries into the death of Mr Knostig.' He couldn't be certain that Helen Blandford hadn't already told him.

It jolted him, so probably she hadn't. But only probably. He looked towards the house and said, 'Jesus Chris'!' but he was another who wasn't going to cry about it. 'The poor bugger. You sure?'

79

There was a long silence while they each waited for the other to say something. Then Wimbush said, ''E was killed?'

'Why do you think that?'

'You wouldn't be 'ere if 'e weren't.' He made that a small triumph of cleverness. Then he shook his head. 'Argh, it don't worry me none. Me an' 'im didn' get on lately.'

'Oh? Why not?'

'None of your bleedin' business, mate, but I didn' want to come one afternoon and 'e said I 'ad to. When I told 'er she said I wasn' to an' I went. When 'e knew 'e told me not to come any more.' He gave a short derisive grunt. 'She told me 'e 'ad no right to and I just stayed on. 'E didn' like me after that, but I didn' 'old no grudge.'

'He wasn't your boss then?'

'No, 'e weren't. 'E thought 'e was, always tellin' me what to do.'

'Was all this because of his drinking?'

'No. 'E'd always done that. Used to come 'ere and 'ave a drink with me sometimes. To get out of 'er way, I reckon.' He scowled, his small mouth downturned. 'And 'e never so much as paid for one of 'em,' he added.

'You mean it was your drink?' To Rogers, he didn't look the sort of man to give anything away.

'Yer. I keep some cans of beer in the shed. It's 'ot work in 'ere, mate.'

'What do you do here? Just this?'

He bristled aggressively at that. 'There ain't no just this, mate. Three days a week and I've got other jobs.'

'I was thinking about outside, the gardens.' He was also thinking that were he not a policeman he could be tempted easily to smack this antagonistic bastard one on his unsavoury chin.

'Not my pigeon,' he said promptly. 'I get paid for in 'ere.'

'Where do you live now?'

He scowled again. 'What you want to know for?'

'Because I'm asking you nice and politely. Where?'

'Nobbers Street,' he almost snarled out. 'In lodgin's.' The secateurs in his hand were being scissored in vicious jerks as though he was mentally cutting into the detective's throat.

'Why do you sleep in the shed?'

'That's my business, mate. I do when I want to.'

'How do you get here from Nobbers Street?'

'I got me van. It's out the back if you want to see it ain't been nicked.'

'Do you ever go into the house?'

'Course I do.' He waved a beefy hand at the plants. 'These 'ere 'ave to feed them insec's. An' I do the waterin' and plantin' in the green'ouse.'

'The one in the laboratory?'

'Yer. There ain't no other.'

'What do you smoke?'

His brain was trying obviously to keep pace with Rogers's changes of course. 'I don't, mate. It ain't good for you.'

'When was the last time you saw Mr Knostig?'

His piggy eyes narrowed in suspicion. 'Las' week sometime. I don' remember. Why do you want to know?'

'Not since?'

He looked at the detective as though he was being trapped in a known lie. 'I saw 'is car,' he said reluctantly.

'When? And where?'

'We'n'sday or Thursday night.' He shook his head. 'No, We'n'sday. I wasn't workin' 'ere that day. I was comin' out of the boozer at chuckin'-out time. The Spread Eagle in 'igh Street,' he said, seeing the question already forming itself on Rogers's mouth.

'He was on his own?'

'I didn' see. I only saw 'is car and it was dark.'

'But it was his car?'

'Yer. I know it anywhere.'

'Which direction was it going?'

''E was goin' in to the Market Square.'

'Do they get many visitors here?'

'Chris'! You want to know the ins and outs of a cat's arse, mate.'

'Yes, I do. Do they?'

'I ain't 'ere 'alf the time.'

'So when you are here.'

'They don'. Except there's that actor feller that comes chasin' after Miss Blan'ford.'

'Humfries?'

'I don' know 'is name. They call 'im Martin.' He leered. 'I bet I know what for an' all.'

'You've got a dirty mind,' Rogers said coldly, but knowing that he was probably right. 'How do you know he's chasing her?'

'She used to go out with 'im, see 'im in the front room. Then they stopped and 'e wasn't let in. Used to knock on the door and the missus'd open it and give 'im the boot.'

'Unpleasantly?'

'She weren't very 'appy about it and 'e used to be mad when 'e came past 'ere. Stan's to reason, dunnit?' He hawked and spat on the soil, not too far from Rogers's shoes but not near enough for him to take open offence. ''E were makin' a bloody nuisance of 'imself.'

'He was a friend of Mr Knostig's as well?'

''Ow would I know, mate? 'E never told me nothin'.' His growing impatience was making him sullen.

'Thanks for being so helpful,' Rogers said straight-faced. 'Hadn't you better get on with your pruning or whatever it is? You've wasted enough time already.'

He turned and walked out of the cage before he could be held to hear Wimbush's spluttered reply. It was a warming feeling to have made a friend, he thought sardonically, even more convinced that the brutish gardener and Mrs Knostig should get together some time and make each other happy in their mutual bloody-mindedness.

15

Lingard had suggested to Rogers that they continue their enquiries in the bar of the Saracen's Head, conveniently situated the width of the street opposite the Police Headquarters. Convenient for them also because, catering as it did to the thirsts of off-duty policemen, there was a marked dearth of customers with guilty consciences and previous convictions to fall gloweringly silent when they entered it.

Leaden and sulphur-yellow clouds, their bellies sagging with water in suspension, loomed towards the town from over the high purple moors as they crossed the street, the air oppressive and sultry, sticking the shirts to their backs. Approaching thunder rumbled like falling rocks in the uneasy hush of an impending storm.

They sat at a table in an unoccupied corner near the exotic fish tank and containers of ferns, pushing away pointedly other chairs near them. Lingard had bought a Pernod for himself and an undiluted whisky for Rogers, the latter asked for as an anaesthetic against the forthcoming smell of the cut-open belly and chest of a man dead for three days. The barman had switched on the lights against the growing gloom and already a few heavy teardrops of rain spattered the window near them.

Lingard had circulated a description of a Wanted for Interrogation Humfries, sent out every available detective on a search of the town – a hue and cry in hot pursuit, he had phrased it to Rogers – and posted one in Humfries' room on the outside chance he might be idiot enough to return for his money, documents and a jacket, all necessary were he to avoid an early arrest. Rogers hadn't hit the ceiling as he had anticipated, had even held back on a frown of displeasure. He must, Lingard had thought, have grown old and mellow prematurely or was replete with a private and splendid satisfaction. His reaction at other times would have been to bellow and drive the CID staff into a turmoil of frenzied activity. It worried Lingard that he hadn't and he remained wary, girded for the delayed fuse ready to burn on an aggravated irritation.

Rogers stared at his second-in-command sipping his milky aniseed drink as though doubting that anybody *compos mentis* could drink the stuff when whisky was available. 'Humfries is too good to be true,' he said. 'It worries me that you didn't find Knostig's bank card. A cheque isn't much good without it. And why tear the cheques out of the book? Writing out a loose cheque isn't the best way to inspire confidence. At its most acceptable, you can only buy goods with it or pay an account, or possibly con a half-wit into changing it. Nobody but a fool would pay out real money on it.'

'You're a wee bit discouraging, George,' Lingard said, not too forcefully. 'He did have nearly the eighty quid Knostig had in his wallet. He's unemployed and should be short of it.'

'True,' Rogers agreed. The illumination from the fish tank gave one side of his face an unsettling saturnine green tinge. 'But that doesn't mean he wouldn't have wodges of it stuffed away. I'm not being cross-grained about it, David, but I'm in a pragmatic mood. He runs away from you, is found in possession of stolen property and is probably living under an assumed name, although that might be because he's an actor. So?' He had seen before what had seemed irrefutable cast-iron evidence of guilt evaporate into nothing by innocent explanation. 'It still leaves me wondering what motive he would have for disposing of poor old lovable Knostig. Why would he wish to make it appear that he'd hared off somewhere by train? Why, having murdered him, would he hang on to some of his property, leave it in his room to be found or to use later to his almost certain detection?' He looked thoughtfully out of the window on pavements streaming with rain. 'He won't last long in this weather anyway. Let's leave the cheques a moment, toss around a more obvious motive. Knostig appears to have had a sexual thing about Helen Blandford. So apparently does Humfries, except that he got chucked. Admittedly, he's a frustrated boyfriend and all that, hanging on to her photograph, sniffing around Nympton Manor.' Rogers didn't like the contemplation of that any more than he could stomach the thought of Knostig having pawed her with his lecherous fingers.

'Which shows her to be a handsome wench, George. I take it she's sexually enticing with it?' He regarded Rogers quizzically, waited for an answer and, when he didn't get it, continued. 'Humfries and Knostig wouldn't exactly love each other. If a turned-on rampant enough Humfries thought that Knostig was trying to dip into his private barrel of honey, that could be motive enough. Particularly if he'd been pitched out in the cold because of it.'

Rain was hissing down now and rattling hard on the window. Thunder cracked overhead and the bar lights dimmed momentarily. Rogers shook his head irritably, waiting for the noise to die away. 'You can't have it both ways,' he growled in the lull. 'If you clobber somebody for taking away your girlfriend, you don't usually steal his wallet as well. At least, I don't think I would. It's usually done in hot blood with violence and Knostig doesn't seem to have a mark on him.' He shook his head again. 'It's a way-out possibility, but not strong enough for me to shut my mind to something more likely.'

'You've latched on to the insect woman?' Lingard murmured, unsquashed and unabashed. 'Because she didn't like her husband or the colour of your eyes?'

'That's right,' Rogers agreed blandly, pushing tobacco into his still-hot pipe. 'I'm latched on to her, on to the Blandford girl, on to Wimbush and your Humfries. I'm even on to Lockersbie and the Reverend Gathercole. If you push me hard enough I'll include the late Mr Harland as well.' He smiled. 'All right, David, you've a point. I'll admit Humfries could be the best bet. So far,' he added cautiously.

'Gad, sir, but that's a generous concession.'

Something else besides the mockery in Lingard's voice made

Rogers say, 'I've trodden on your sensibilities, David, but I'm only giving you back your own Devil's Advocate stuff.' He stood. 'I'll get another round.'

When he returned from the bar counter with the drinks he still held his wallet in his hand. He laid it by the side of his whisky and sat. 'Perish the thought, David,' he said, 'but were you my wife, would you expect to know how much money I have in that?'

Lingard pinched snuff into his nostrils and sniffed. 'As a quite happy bachelor I sometimes wonder why you lot bother with marriage. No, I wouldn't,' he said hastily, seeing the beginning of a frown on Rogers's face.

'No, it's unlikely you would. But Mrs Knostig did and she was barely on speaking terms with him. We don't have many reservations with our wives and mistresses but one of them is, I feel, how much we happen to have in our wallets. You don't say "Darling, for your information I've £80 in my wallet". That would be dangerous, and I think not.'

'It's not much to go on, is it?'

'No, it damned well isn't. All I have that isn't speculation is that she didn't like him, Helen Blandford didn't, Humfries probably didn't and I'm certain Wimbush didn't. Poor old unwanted Knostig,' he said feelingly. 'Apart from his being dead, I feel sorry for him. He hadn't got much to live for.' He looked at his watch and grimaced. 'Talking of not being in good odour, I've Bridget waiting at the mortuary for me. You finish your drink in peace and come up with something brilliant by the time I get back.'

Walking across the street in the lashing rain with a senior police officer's *gravitas* which forbade him scurrying, he knew that he wasn't looking forward at all to Bridget's continuing hostility and wondering what he could bend himself to do about it.

Splashing through the rain because an ambulance blocked his car's passage to the hospital's entrance, Rogers felt the familiar frisson of nausea as he approached what he knew would be an hour or two of watching the bloody decanting of a corpse. No murder, or suspected murder, committed within his bailiwick could be properly investigated without his personal attendance, only rarely delegated to an immediate subordinate, at the surgical search for or confirmation of the cause of death. It wasn't ever what he could consider the gratification of an anatomical curiosity as Bridget did, and it reminded him morbidly that it might, one day, be done to him.

Walking the unlighted brick tunnel leading to the basement mortuary, his footfalls echoing an invisible follower, he passed the refrigerated green drawers containing the wards' daily discharge of lost patients into the subterranean limbo, sensing the – to him – tangible aura of brooding death, capable of filling his mind with melancholia.

He pushed open the swing doors into the formalin-smelling, brightly-lit interior of metal cabinets and working-tops, shelves of glass jars and enamel bowls of preserved organs and a terrazzo floor slopping with antisepticized water. Bridget, already dressed in a khaki-green gown and a red plastic apron, a linen cap covering her hair, was pulling on thin rubber gloves that would protect her hands from the bacilli in decaying flesh. The bad odour in which Rogers had found himself at the churchyard had not dissipated and showed in the brief nod with which she acknowledged his appearance.

The naked body of Knostig lay face-upwards on one of the stainless-steel necropsy tables, bathed in the shadowless light of the lamps hanging above. It glistened from the pre-examination sluicing, showing every contour and crease in sharp relief. The features, cleaned of soil, had been composed to the non-expression of a quiet death although lopsided, and Rogers could identify him with the photograph he had been given. The legs, now unconcealed from civilizing trousers, were unusually thick with hair and went ill with his middle-class citizen's face. Almost, the detective thought, as though he really had been the goatish satyr described by Helen Blandford. Water dribbled around him from a green hose, running into a drain grill at his feet. The pads of his fingers and thumbs were stained black where his prints had been taken. The clothes removed from him, folded and packaged in polythene, had been placed on an adjacent working-top.

One of Rogers's scenes-of-crime men was taking photographs, recording every aspect of the body before it was ravaged by Bridget's scalpels. When he had finished and left them, Bridget – having waited in an uncomfortable silence – tied a cotton mask over her nose and mouth, leaving only her orange eyes for Rogers to talk at. Then she selected her instruments from a wall cabinet and moved to the side of the body.

'Not a nice day, Bridget,' Rogers said conversationally as he sat himself on a working-top in his still-wet raincoat. It was a banal remark but he had to start somewhere.

'No,' she replied.

'It's raining.'

'So I've noticed,' she said drily, adjusting a microphone suspended at mouth level over the table. 'Would you mind switching on the tape recorder?'

He had to get off the working-top to do it and realized that he was beginning to feel fatigued from his sleepless night. And that always irritated him as a weakness. Reseating himself, he said, 'I see what you mean about the hypostasis. He died face downwards?'

'Either that or he was turned on to it shortly afterwards. Enough for the blood to have drained into the frontal aspect.' She was brusque, not looking around to him. 'The contact flattening suggests quite definitely it was on a hard surface.'

'Like the ground?'

'Like anything not soft such as a settee or a bed; anything unyielding enough to produce a uniform flattening. Even, as you can see, on one side of the face.'

'How long would he need to be in that position?' He knew the answers to much of what he was asking but they had to be pronounced by the pathologist. Occasionally post-mortem symptoms dispensed with natural logic and processes.

'Eight to twelve hours. But it could be less.' ·

'He was seen in a sitting position, legs outstretched, in the church porch about twenty-four hours after death. Is that consistent with the onset of rigor mortis?'

'It isn't relevant. Stiffening almost certainly took place during the time he lay dead on his stomach.' She was holding Knostig's head steady with spread fingers and positioning the blade of her scalpel under the chin. She put pressure on it and Rogers swallowed, averting his eyes. Illogically, the first cut into the soft flesh of the throat was the worst for him. He had a persisting horror that there could be an occasion when the eyelids would snap open and the mouth scream in awakened shock. But he couldn't close his ears to the sound of flesh being sliced down through the chest to the belly by the same hands that had so often made tactile love to the same parts of himself. He had had occasional unsettling difficulties in keeping the two activities separate in his mind.

Bridget was speaking when he returned his gaze to what she was doing. 'Stiffening would normally be established in about ten hours,' she said, 'but anyway there's no great difficulty in breaking the rigor. And once it's broken it won't reappear.'

'He had to be taken somehow to the churchyard. There'd be no problems about fitting him into a car?' The smell was reaching him and he refilled and lit his pipe against its intrusion into his throat. Without Lingard's snuff being available his nose would have to look after itself.

'None at all, given the need.' With the flesh laid back she was snipping deftly through the exposed ribs with bone shears.

He sat in silence, feeling shut out, smoking fiercely and watching her as she extracted, sliced and examined each component part of the dead man's chest cavity, speaking each condition of it into the microphone. Listening, Rogers could decipher enough of her medicalese to understand that Knostig had died neither from the ingress of a foreign body into an organ nor from any disease of the cardio-vascular system. She appeared to be less definite about the presence of any indication of asphyxia, though certain that there were no accidental impactions of substances in the larynx, trachea or bronchi, no signs of homicidal suffocation or strangling. There was, it seemed, a slight oedema of the lungs. 'An effusion of a watery nature into the interstices of the tissues,' she explained as an apparent aside for his understanding. She added that it did not, standing on its own, mean much at the moment.

When she removed the stomach, laying it on the table and scissoring open its membranous bag, she murmured 'Agh' and spoke to him directly. 'There's some staining of the mucous membrane. Not much, but probably significant.'

'Significant of what, Bridget?'

'That it could be caused by a strong irritant or a mild corrosive.'

'You mean a poison?'

'When I do I'll say so.' She lifted the mask from her mouth and nose with a rubbered finger and sniffed at the stomach's interior, straightening and shaking her head. 'I don't know, it needs a laboratory analysis. Possibly I shall be able to give you an opinion when I've finished.'

Rogers was disappointed, for she had a nose for olfactory identification as another might have for vintage wines. 'Could the dilation of the pupils you mentioned be connected?' he asked.

'It might. Then again, it might not. It certainly needs more support than this staining.' She was everting the stomach and he wished she wouldn't, even with rubber gloves on.

'Is that stuff there his last meal?'

'What's left of it, and don't ask me what he ate, it's much too masticated.'

'Can it indicate how long after it he died? It could be important.'

She was impatient with him, which was unusual even in her worst moods. She was still simmering over something. 'No, it can't. It's variable, depending on what he ate; its fat content and moistness, for example. But all things being average – and they seldom are – it takes about two or three hours for it to begin to move into the duodenum.' She shrugged. 'Thereafter it depends on its quantity, its resistance to the gastric juices and the activity or otherwise of the digestive system.'

'And anything he drank?'

'It would filter through the kidneys and into the bladder almost immediately. And that's empty.'

'Perhaps the poor bugger died of dehydration,' he said with an attempt at humour which fell flat from no response. For a woman with whom he had been to bed she was being stonily intractable, making it impossible for him to even begin to penetrate her reserve. But they were, he had to admit, supposed to be totally immersed in their work, although only automatons could be so fortunate.

Decanting the belly, she spoke only to the microphone, her unresponsive back to him. Finishing with the trunk she plugged in the oscillating necropsy saw and began her examination of the head.

'There's some evidence of oedema here,' she said after a long period of silence during which he had forced his thinking away from her bloody-mindedness. 'Not much, but useful. The aggregated symptoms might support a form of poisoning. There's certainly nothing else, and anything I say now is subject to the results of chemical analysis.'

She was taking the pieces of each organ she had put aside and dropping them into separate glass jars, sealing them with rubber stoppers. From now on they would be Rogers's responsibility, required to be cherished as much as if they had been taken from his own body. He winced at the indignities a murdered body was required to suffer at the hands of a pathologist and promised himself that he would die a natural death. The thought of Bridget or anybody else doing this to him, his pudenda exposed to curious eyes, was an unhappy one.

'Dammit, Bridget,' he growled, 'that'll be forever.' It was frustrating him. The filtering, distillation and testing needed to identify a poison took lengthy time-wasting days at the Forensic Science Laboratory, even when it wasn't waiting in the queue with exhibits for examination from other police forces.

'So it will.' She had pulled her mask down and was stripping off her gloves. 'I'm not a toxicologist so don't take it as a fact, but I'll plump for poisoning. In the negative sense, not a metallic poison such as antimony, mercury or arsenic or any of the barbiturates or hypnotics. At a pinch, although I don't think so, it could be sodium fluoride or cyanide.' She pursed her lips in doubt. 'I don't know, but it leaves me with something like a vegetable poisoning. At least, the symptoms don't negate it.'

He was feeling aggrieved at Knostig for not dying of something explicable, but'if it had been poison he thought it a harsh retribution for a bit of female-groping or whatever the reason. 'I need more, Bridget,' he said. 'Such as what?'

Sliding from the working-top, he moved to where she was scrubbing her hands pink in steaming water at a wash-basin.

'Think about it,' she said offhandedly. 'We're surrounded by them and God knows they're common enough. You'll find poisons in laburnum, yew and laurel. Toadstools I imagine you'll know about. Then there is deadly nightshade, hemlock, even green potatoes. And there are plenty of others. Think about this. Some of them contain the alkaloid atropine which dilates the pupils. Some of them *don't* have it but still do, so don't let that mislead you.'

'Would it include alcohol poisoning? He was supposed to be a heavy drinker.' Damn her! Why did she have to look so attractive, even bundled up in that shapeless gown?

'Not heavy enough for his liver to be cirrhotic. Nor was there any congestion of the brain or odour in the stomach.'

'He ate some duck pâté just before he left home. Could that be significant?'

She thought about it. 'If it's bacterial poisoning you're suggesting, I'm sure he would have taken longer to die. Poisoning from salmonella usually results in acute enteritis – diarrhoea and vomiting – and there's no evidence of that. Botulism isn't so easy to diagnose because it kills by respiratory paralysis.' She made a small gesture of irritation. 'It's the laboratory's job and you'll have to suggest it in your report.'

'Without committing yourself, how happy are you with vegetable poisoning?' he said doggedly. By God, but she was a difficult woman, and she made him feel that he was, by comparison, reasonableness itself.

'Enough not to chance using up the specimens by examining them myself. Were I you, I'd be happy enough to accept it as a working hypothesis, but not cry your eyes out if the laboratory says differently.'

Bridget possessed a true medical caution but, without committing herself, was telling him to go ahead on her diagnosis. 'Yes,' he said, not too disgruntled at what he realized was all he was going to get. 'I'll do that.'

Undoing the tapes of her gown, she walked into the changing room and Rogers followed her. It was as though she were undressing for him. Beneath the gown and apron she now removed she wore a professionally-grey skirt matching the soberness of his own suit, a dark-blue shirt with pens and a bleeper in the breast pocket. With the door closed and the terrible odour of death shut out, he could smell her scent and, with the final releasing of her copper hair from the surgeon's cap, see a more feminine woman.

'When can I expect your report, Bridget?' he asked. It was something to say to prolong his being with her, although he couldn't see much of a future in it.

She turned from bundling the cast clothing into a plastic bin, her eyes angry. 'Damn you and your report!' she burst out fiercely. 'Don't you want to know where I was this morning?'

He was taken aback, for he hadn't thought about it. 'If you want to tell me.'

'I'm on the short list for an appointment as senior pathologist in Norfolk and I was being interviewed for it here.'

It was quiet enough for him to hear the hose still running water in the next room. 'That's a blow for me,' he said inadequately, for it had shaken him. 'You're serious?'

'Of course I'm serious. Why shouldn't I be?' Her eyes held his, challenging him on something. She had never looked more desirable than in this moment of threatened loss.

It was a hard thing to do but he smiled to hide his dismay. 'I was always expecting that you'd be cutting me up if I met a violent end. That's always been a comfort to me,' he lied. 'I wouldn't like a stranger to do it.'

'Don't fool yourself.' Her anger had receded, apparently seeing in him what she wanted to. 'You'd be sold off to a pork butcher.'

'Yes,' he said, 'I probably would. You're not taking it, are you?'

'It matters to you?'

'Of course it bloody matters. I don't want to lose you.' Beneath all his confusion of being still married, being subject to inhibiting Police Regulations, his own moral integrity – admittedly bruised, but still viable – and his suspicion that what he felt for her wasn't love, he knew he didn't want her to go, that he needed her. Just what for he couldn't be sure, but his darker self, looking over his shoulder, reminded him that she had a beautiful body sheathed with a remarkably creamy skin.

'Sometimes I hate you, George. You're still the same blow-hot, blow-cold Rogers you've always been.'

'It's because I've a brother called Guilt.' He was gentle with her. 'Not that it alters either of us. I'm me – flawed and married me, if you like. You're you and disturbing to me in the nicest way.'

They heard the sound of somebody entering the mortuary. 'That will be the porter,' she said, 'and he'll certainly think you're in here helping me to get dressed and taking advantage of me.' She hesitated as he moved towards the door. 'Don't run away, George. We could have a sherry in my room.' That had been a regular post-mortem examination ritual.

'And you'll tell me you're not going?' he pressed her, telling himself that Knostig and his problems were not going to decamp anyway during a short absence from them.

'I haven't got it yet,' she said, 'and it depends.' Which sounded remarkably like a warning to him.

16

While Bridget took the staff lift Rogers, his raincoat over his arm and trying to appear as though he was visiting a patient, traversed the claustrophobic ward corridors and climbed stairs where he could be seen without medical foreheads being creased. He disliked the smells and sounds of suffering human-ity no less than those of the mortuary. The whiffs of floor polish and antiseptics, crisp nurses carrying bowls with hypodermic syringes destined for sticking into shrinking buttocks, white-coated doctors scurrying to what he was certain must be to mortal relapses and unforeseen arrests of breathing, were no repudiations of his mortuary-induced belief in the transitori-ness of life.

He countered it by trying to work out who the hell would wish to poison Knostig, which gave him the comforting assur-ance that he was still working on it, still more or less on duty. He didn't wish to carry too many guilts around with him.

The climb to the top floor of the hospital had given his lungs a beating and he made one of his unmeant resolves to cut down on his smoking. Without knocking, he opened the door to Bridget's apartment and slipped in, he hoped without being seen. There was no Bridget and he could hear the sounds of spraying water in the shower.

It was a small room with large windows, partially obstructed by rampantly growing pot plants, that gave a bird's-eye view of the hospital car park and, beyond the roofs and chimney stacks of the town, a panorama of very wet moorland overhung by pewter clouds. The hopsack-covered chairs were comfortably cushioned, the shaggy brown carpet spongy as meadow turf. A sideboard of books on forensic medicine and a length of wired-together human vertebrae that looked like the skeleton of a snake gave the room, he thought satirically, a homely touch. By the books were two bottles of a pale sherry and glasses.

He poured out two glasses of it, taking his to a window and, as he waited, examining and fingering the unfamiliar leaves of the plants, wondering which of them might contain toxins noxious to the human digestion.

When Bridget emerged she was pink and glowing and wrapped not too tightly in a white towelling robe. With her feet bare she was manifestly naked beneath it. There was no smile, no coquetry, nothing in her manner to suggest invitation, the expression in her eyes neutral. He could have been somebody who had happened unexpectedly into her apartment while she was taking a shower.

He handed her the sherry he had poured, not certain whether her near nakedness or his earlier dwelling on the eroticism of Helen Blandford was the catalyst to the rise in his sexual temperature. But it was there and he decided on masculine initiative, putting his arm around her waist and pulling her to him. When he kissed her, tasting the sherry on her lips, she responded by curving her body hard against his.

'Blow-hot Rogers in the ascendant,' she said mockingly into his mouth. While she smelled sensuously of perfumed soap and powder, he knew that his clothing must reek of the microscopic particles of Knostig that had floated about in the mortuary. Nothing in her expression showed that she was conscious of it, but its possibility could be a valid reason for getting out of it.

'You must have spiked the sherry,' he said solemnly.

She pushed free from him and emptied her glass, then walking into her bedroom and leaving the door open, though only just open. It was now all up to him and he knew that to follow her would be to concede a sort of defeat. He thought – not too lengthily – of the impermanence of the flesh, regretting missed opportunities, and what would be an unwarranted absence from a murder enquiry. Having lost a night's sleep and believing his skull to be packed with damp cottonwool, he was not in the best condition for impromptu love but, recognizing the unforgivable when he saw it, he took a deep breath and followed her. *Homo sapiens erectus running amok*, he told himself, *and it's been far too long*.

Resting with her in the disordered bedclothing, the room twilit from drawn curtains, and feeling her warm breath moist on his chest, he said, 'I've been thinking, Bridget. Assuming that Knostig *was* put down with a vegetable poison, how would it be extracted?' He didn't wish her to think him wholly wrapped up in her needs or attempting to influence her decision on moving.

She bit him hard and he grunted. 'Damn you, Rogers. Don't tell me that you're null and void so soon.'

He thought he was, and that part of his mind not engaged in re-attending to the extravagances of their bodies pondered on whether it could be counted a moral dishonesty for him to enter in his desk diary, *General Hospital, 2.30 p.m. Conference with Dr B. J. Hunter, pathologist, re death of R. Knostig.*

17

Lingard, having completed the enquiries Rogers had allocated to him and wondering why the post-mortem examination of Knostig was taking so long, waited at his superior's desk for his return. He stared with distaste at the rain lashing against the window glass, wanting to get on with something in Rogers's absence but not knowing what.

On the blotting-pad in front of him were documents he had collated. A photocopy of an entry in the previous week's *Post and Messenger* revealed an interesting item of information that among the otherwise unknown mourners at the burial of Charles Harland in the churchyard of Saint Boniface was a Mr A. Wimbush, nephew of the deceased.

A telephone message from the Forensic Science Laboratory identified the film of liquid scraped from the floor of the church porch as probable vomit similar in colour and density to the drops of it found on the rear flooring of Knostig's Citroën. It would be analysed for its constituents after the weekend.

A batch of reports resulting from the house-to-house enquiries made in the vicinity of the churchyard had nothing in them to indicate that on the night of Lockersbie's finding of the body any householder had seen a parked car or flitting lights among the graves, heard the sounds of digging or even noted the unconcealed arrival and departure of Lockersbie.

A delayed report from a night-duty P.C. – 106 Wates – who had since been on a rest period was a little more helpful. At about 2.40 a.m. the same night he had seen a Citroën Safari, index number and colour unobtained in the darkness and with no reason to note either, being driven along Colbourne Street in the direction of the railway station. When it approached a distant street lamp, he had seen momentarily the silhouette of the driver. His impression was that it was a male, but he could not be certain.

A folder of still-damp photographs of Knostig being exhumed showed nothing that Lingard and Rogers had not seen for themselves, although one did include a chance shot of Rogers and the Reverend Gathercole being unhappy with each other. With the folder was a blown-up photograph of Humfries which Lingard had already put in hand for printing and circulating to Divisions and adjacent police forces. That he was dressed as a pantomime Prince Charming was a necessity born of the fact that it had been the only portrait found in his room and Lingard suspected that Rogers was not going to approve.

The telephone numbers found in Knostig's pocket had been checked out and were those of a firm of solicitors, an estate agent and a financial broker known to Lingard by his advertisements offering loans at a usurious interest. The number reversed was anomalous, being that of a health food shop in the town's Market Square.

Lingard's own report was there of his second interview with Mrs Cunninghame, from which he had just returned at the sacrifice of his lunch. She could now recall that Humfries occasionally left the house late at night. She could not be certain, her memory not being at its best, but he had gone out shortly before midnight on either Wednesday or Thursday – the nights of Knostig's death and his subsequent burial, although Lingard hadn't mentioned that aspect of his enquiry to her. She had not heard him return because she had gone to sleep after his departure. As he was a handsome young man with, no doubt, lots of young ladies to see and was always back in bed in the morning, she had not thought it any of her business.

Lingard thought it not too bad a couple of hours' squirrelling, a useful something to set against his losing Humfries; a carelessness which still niggled at his psyche and left him feeling that when he did catch up with the slippery actor he was going to be extremely terse with him.

He was paring his already immaculate fingernails with a penknife, certain that Rogers had got himself caught up in something complicated and irritating to the spirit and hoping that he wasn't going to pass it on, when the telephone bell rang. He lifted the receiver and answered 'Lingard here', telling the Enquiry Office Sergeant that Mr Rogers was out. 'I've a man here, sir,' the sergeant said, 'who says his name is Humfries and that he wants to give himself up. He's a bit shy about saying what for.'

Humfries, standing with his back against the Enquiry Office

counter, was sodden from the rain, his hair flat on his head in spiky wisps, his shirt a dark yellow and pasted to his skin and the now shapeless trousers dripping puddles of water on to the floor tiles. Despite his soaking there was nothing abject about him, but an almost defiant jauntiness that didn't quite hide the wariness in his eyes as he watched Lingard approach. He straightened himself, holding up an open hand and said 'Shalom.'

'You forgot to take your mackintosh, old son,' Lingard said smiling. He thought that he might get on with this apparently agreeable-in-defeat man and his intention to terseness was discarded.

'It was daft of me.' He smiled back; a relieved smile as though he had anticipated being jumped on and frogmarched unceremoniously into a cell. 'I'd no money either and nowhere to go. I also had a bad attack of a conscience, wanting to get it off my chest.' He looked contrite. 'I'm sorry you fell over. I hope you weren't hurt.'

'Let's go to my office and talk about it. I'll get you a towel.'

'That's decent of you, though I don't deserve it.' His voice had the resonant delivery of an actor accustomed, Lingard supposed, to pitching it at a comatose audience in the back rows.

He walked behind his prisoner, shepherding him up the stairs and watchful, despite his surrender, against any change of mind and attempt at escape. It had happened before with the sudden transition from freedom into custody, with the first smell of deflating confinement, and no police officer had yet contrived an acceptable excuse for allowing it to happen.

In his office, Lingard locked the door and pocketed the key. 'Not that I think you would, old son,' he said amiably, 'but I warn you that trying to could be extremely painful.' He took a towel from a cupboard and tossed it to him. 'Sit while you're doing it. I'll send for a change of gear after we've had our little chat.'

'Now,' he said, sitting and switching on the tape recorder in the drawer of the desk, 'I think some explanations are in order. First, what is your name? Not Humfries, I assume?' He gave his mind to a policeman's detailed appraisal of the features of a man he needed to know and remember. His pale-grey eyes still held an apprehensive wariness, his nose was short and indicated stubbornness. His mouth, although pleasant, was soft and pink and suggested a contrary weakness. He was, Lingard considered a little uncharitably, the sort likely to be scooped up by an older dominant woman and to be only too willing to perform for his keep.

'Horace Pritt,' he answered, not sounding as if he liked it much. 'Martin Humfries is my stage name and I prefer to be known by it.'

'And you're out of work at the moment?'

'I'm in between engagements. It happens in my profession.'

'I imagine I know why you ran, but you tell me.'

'The cheques, of course.' He looked surprised, the towel he was using held poised. 'Why else? I mean, it was so unexpected. I thought at first you were a bloke from the theatre. When you weren't and said you were a policeman I just panicked, I suppose.' He grinned. 'I knew it wouldn't last long.'

'That's a built-in anxiety with villains.' Lingard pinched snuff and inhaled it into his nostrils, hesitating, then offering the open box to Humfries.

The actor shook his head. 'No, thank you. It gives me catarrh.'

Lingard closed the box and slid it back into his waistcoat pocket. He hadn't relished the prospect of damp fingers fumbling in it anyway. 'What does stealing cheques from Mr Knostig give you, old son?'

He blinked. 'Stealing? That's a strong word. I borrowed them without his permission. I admit that, but then I have no choice, have I?'

Lingard held his gaze without speaking, reminding himself that this man was an actor and professionally capable of deceiving with his emotions and facial expressions, the boyish features predestined by human fallibility to hide a wickedness or two. He wasn't convinced by miles of the motives for his surrender. His running away had given him time to sort out what kind of a story he was going to pitch.

'Stealing from a dead man,' he said with deliberation. 'From Richard Knostig, maliciously murdered, unlawfully buried and his cheque book stolen feloniously from his body.'

A succession of overemphasized emotions followed each other across his face as though he were trying each out for suitability and he half-rose from his chair. 'He's dead! Christ, you don't mean it . . . I didn't, I swear I didn't! You think I did!' The words tumbled out from a shaking mouth.

'*Sit down!*' Lingard snapped at him and he subsided, a damp bag of hunted wretchedness with his jauntiness gone. The detective waited, allowing the silence to lengthen until its tautness became uncomfortable. 'Did you?' he asked, searching his eyes for the answer and not getting it.

'No,' he said dully, 'I didn't even know he was dead . . . poor bastard.'

'You don't appear to resent my thinking you might have.'

'No. It's your job, I suppose, but I didn't.'

'All right, old son, if you say so.' Lingard had decided to adopt the attitude of appearing to be satisfied that he hadn't. It encouraged garrulity in peripheral matters. He held the three cheques between finger and thumb. 'These,' he said. 'Tell me how.'

'I borrowed them, honestly I did. They're worth nothing really. The banks don't charge for them. I tore them out from the back of his cheque book.'

'Where and when?'

'In his house about three weeks ago. I was there visiting someone and while I was there waiting I saw his book on the bureau. I needed a cheque so I took them.'

'That sounds a mite thin to me, old son. These have his name printed on them. Richard Francis Knostig, not Martin Humfries or Horace Pritt.'

'I didn't think of that when I took them.' He grimaced. 'Even that's a pretty despicable thing to do, isn't it?'

'Yes, and it still amounts to a theft. Was he a friend?'

'A sort of half-and-half. There were things about him I didn't like.'

'Such as?'

'Personal matters which I'm sure wouldn't interest you.' He had reacted as if an exposed nerve had been touched.

'Everything about you interests me, old son, and I don't wish to have to drag it out of you bit by bit.' Lingard was deep in doubt about his sincerity, his initial liking for him evaporating. He tapped his finger on the desk, making his voice stern. 'If I'm going to convince my chief that you've nothing to do with Knostig's murder you'll have to be a lot more forthcoming. I know you have – or had – an association with Miss Blandford and you took the cheques from where she lives, so suppose we start from that while I sit and listen.'

He thought about that, his forehead wrinkled and taking more time than Lingard considered even a guilt-stricken penitent should. When he spoke it was patently in the role of the misunderstood leading man, his abjection put to one side and an earnest frankness in the face of adversity taking its place.

'She loved me and I was in love with her,' he said as though it explained everything. 'I still am. I used to see her at Nympton Manor and that's how I came to know Richard and his wife. It was always difficult, you know, in somebody else's house. I don't run a car now and I can't entertain in lodgings.' He twitched his mouth jerkily and added deprecatingly, 'I've only me and that wasn't enough. Not that Richard had anything to do with that, although Helen did tell me that he'd had a go at her. I mean, that dirty old lecher. You know, cock-happy, living in the same house and not getting it from his wife. You'd think he was past it at his age. Not that I was jealous of him, although he probably was of me. I didn't like it, but Helen seemed to think it all a bit of a scream and found it amusing.'

'The cheques,' Lingard reminded him. 'We've rather wandered away from those, haven't we?'

'I'm sorry, I thought I'd explained that. I was waiting in the sitting-room for Helen one evening – we were going to the theatre – and I saw this cheque book. It was on a Saturday and I was out of cheques and needing one.' He grimaced, his fingers pulling at the fabric of his wet shirt. 'We're none of us perfect and we do stupid things on occasion. I thought it could be Helen's and I knew she wouldn't mind. Once I'd torn them out and realized they were Richard's it was too late. I couldn't very well put them back so I just shoved them in my pocket. If you say that's stealing them then I'll have to plead guilty and take my medicine.'

'What a pity we have neither Knostig alive nor his cheque book with us to confirm it,' Lingard said without expression. 'That must have occurred to you. Why did you keep them hidden in your drawer?'

'God knows. I thought it would be wrong to tear them up.'

'You didn't use one? You said that you needed a cheque.' Lingard was less an interrogator, more an inquisitive friend casually interested in his doings while being grateful that liars did occasionally get confused.

'Of course not. It wasn't possible with his name all over the dam' things.' That had been another exposed nerve and he dodged away from it. 'But I hadn't finished telling you about Helen.'

'My fault, old son. I wanted the cheque business cleared up.' He beamed encouragingly. 'I understand she hasn't been so friendly lately?'

Humfries scowled. 'No, she hasn't. It's that bloody woman's doing, Olivia Knostig. She's got Helen completely obsessed with her. I'd suspected it for some time, but I suppose it seemed not to matter so much with a couple of women. Helen follows her around like a bloody lapdog. And conversely cooling off on me. On *me*,' he said, his expression reflecting the absurd inexplicableness of it. 'She's butch, she must be, and Helen's fool enough to be taken in by her. She's not the same girl – it's revolting, disgusting, and they probably sleep together.'

'Dented pride might exaggerate it,' Lingard murmured, though not disbelieving it. 'Women can be a little more innocently chummy together than we males.'

'No'. He was vehement. 'I saw them in the garden only last week, holding hands and looking at each other like a couple of bitches on heat. They made me want to puke. No,' he qualified, 'not Helen. But *she* did.'

'You were hiding in a bush?'

'I was looking through the gate,' he said stiffly. 'I'm bloody well *persona non grata* with Mrs Knostig. I can't even speak to Helen on the telephone. If that she-dragon answers – and she always does – she tells me Helen's not available and bangs down on me.'

Lingard decided on a small unlosable gamble, turning over a page of his notes and ostensibly reading. 'You were up at Nympton Manor late on Wednesday – or was it Thursday?'

Humfries was startled. 'How the hell would you know that?'

'You could have been seen. It was Thursday, wasn't it?' He saw the unwitting confirmation in his eyes. 'Of course it was. What were you doing there?'

'I was telephoning Helen.'

'At midnight?' He remembered that there was a kiosk in the road, apparently unvandalized. 'Why from up there?'

'I knew she'd be in at that time and I could see the windows of the bedrooms from there. If she'd answered I would have seen the light switched on, seen whether she was in her own room or in Mrs Knostig's.'

'Cunning fella, but you must have been a bit of a damned nuisance,' Lingard said. 'And you don't necessarily switch on a light to answer the telephone. Did she answer?'

'No, nobody did.'

'No lights about?'

'Nothing.'

Lingard couldn't be sure, but Humfries' eyes held all the

sincerity and frankness of a man who was lying through his teeth. 'Was Knostig's car outside the house?'

'I wouldn't know. I didn't look.'

'Why were you so long away from your lodgings?' A loaded question because he didn't know.

Humfries frowned at that. 'Who said I was? I went back straight away. What else could I do?' he said bitterly. 'Mrs Cunninghame can tell you if she wasn't asleep.'

'Or if you didn't take off your shoes and creep in.'

'I'd no need to. I came straight back.' That had offended him, but there was an air of confidence in his voice that suggested to Lingard he was pressing the wrong button.

'When was the last time you spoke to Knostig? Or saw him?'

'You know about that, too, I suppose?' When Lingard didn't answer, holding his eyes unblinkingly, he said, 'The previous evening. I was going to tell you anyway. I was having a drink at the Minster Hotel and he came into the bar.'

When he didn't enlarge on it, Lingard said, 'So? Expand. Don't just send me telegrams.'

'I'm trying to help, but you're confusing me about what I should say.'

'Innocence pleads to speak, old son, but guilt holds its tongue,' Lingard quoted affably. 'Jeremy Bentham said that and I'm passing it on.'

'Richard came into the bar and saw me, came over straight away. I thought Judas wept, he knows I took his cheques and is looking for me. But he apparently wasn't. He just said Hello and sat next to me and I bought him a drink. He asked for a double brandy which I thought was a bit hot. Then when he got it he filled the glass up with soda-water. Dying of thirst, he said. He was acting as if he'd had more than a few . . . well, I don't suppose I should say it now that he's dead, but he was sloshed to the eyeballs. He was wobbling about on his stool and prattling on about nothing much.' He jerked his head in sudden realization. 'Christ! Is that when he was murdered? I mean, afterwards?'

'Let's stick to what you know.' Lingard had never believed he was in the business of giving out information. 'What was the nothing much he was talking about?'

'I was only listening with half an ear. I didn't exactly welcome his company.' He grinned knowingly in a man-to-man understanding. 'I was more interested in a smashing popsy further along who I'd been hoping to chat up. Anyway, it was rambling stuff about him making a big mistake – no, two big mistakes in his life, without actually saying what they were. And he kept repeating something about that bloody obstinate bitch. He obviously meant his wife, because she is. Bitch! Bitch! he kept muttering. Actually, I don't think he was saying it to me, sort of . . . well, to himself. Whatever, he wasn't very happy and at one time his eyes were all pink. All dreadfully embarrassing. I thought he might be going to blub and that's why I was sure he was tight. Apart from him not being very good company, I was still worried about the cheques and I pushed off as soon as I decently could. It was near enough closing time anyway and the popsy had gone.'

'It didn't occur to you that he might have wanted to confide in you?'

'Not really. Why should he?'

There had to be more but Lingard knew that a little at a time paid accumulated dividends at the end. 'The double brandy you bought him shouldn't have hurt you,' he said offhandedly. 'Not with £75 or more in your wallet. And, 'pon my soul, you haven't been working for a month.'

Humfries' eyes slanted away from the detective's, his mouth working wordlessly, any acting he had been doing deserting him and with Lingard almost smelling the guilt. When he spoke he was struggling to affect a casual sincerity. 'Unemployment benefit,' he got out. 'I . . . I had some saved, of course.'

'Coincidentally, Knostig had £80 stolen from his wallet. Together with the cheque book from which these cheques came.' Lingard was no longer affable, his blue eyes daunting. 'While he was dead, too. No doubt we could find his fingerprints on the notes. We use a chemical called Ninhydrin, in case you doubt we can,' he added.

'No, you won't . . . you can't.'

'If you say so. Anyway, stealing from a corpse amounts only to simple theft with a maximum of ten years,' he said comfortingly. 'That shouldn't worry you when you're getting very close to being charged with murder. And even if you didn't steal it from him, you certainly didn't get it from . . .' He tailed off, for Humfries was staring hypnotically at the cheques on the desk.

'Well, well,' the detective murmured. 'You avaricious little sod. Where did you learn to forge signatures?'

Humfries' throat agitated as he tried to swallow and he shook his head dumbly.

'A bit more serious that. Uttering a forged document is punishable on indictment with up to fourteen years in chokey,' Lingard amplified helpfully. 'It's got to be one or the other, hasn't it?' He waited, watching the struggles of a man who had inadvertently walked into a pit of snakes and was seeking a way out.

'You are what they call on the horns of a dilemma, aren't you?' he said when nothing came. 'Not knowing whether to admit to stealing from a dead man or to confess to forging his signature on a cheque. Or, of course, doing both.'

Humfries groaned and found words. 'I have to think . . . I'm confused,' he said.

'I'm sure you are.' Lingard was beginning to feel sorry for him and that was a spoiler to incisive interrogation. It would help to defer it, to wait for it to wear off and give him time to do some checking with the bank which would, anyway, be closed for the weekend. It would come from Humfries eventually and all the sooner for brooding alone on the inescapable. 'In the meantime,' he said, 'I'm going to charge you with the theft of cheque forms from the late Richard Knostig and tuck you up in a cell to do your thinking.' He rose from his chair and retrieved the door key from his pocket. 'Come on, old son, and get out of your wet clobber. Take comfort from the fact that they don't hang and gibbet you for it these days.'

18

Rogers, standing at the window of his office, stared morosely at the scene below him. With the rain clouds gone and the sun drying the puddled traffic-choked streets, steam rose from the roof tiles of the brown brick and dingy masonry hemming in the unlovely concrete and glass of Police Headquarters. The sun should have lifted his spirits, but it hadn't. Lingard had told him of his interview with Humfries and fed him the information he had collated. None of that had put dancing laughter in his eyes either. He was irritated with himself – and by definition with everybody else – for needing to nurse a guilt. He felt that it hadn't been the done thing. Not in prosaic raining daylight; not when any dedicated and conscientious Detective Superintendent should have been concentrating his intellectual regard on murder. Worse, he suspected that he carried visibly on himself the stigmata of Bridget's love-making and that Lingard would recognize it. Not even knowing that all over the world other men and women must also be doing it helped. Perhaps not in the course of investigating a murder, but even that couldn't be unique. It just felt that way. And it had proved to be more therapeutic than rhapsodic and a weakness he should have overcome.

'Don't you feel that the bloody fates are still conspiring against us, David?' he asked. 'Bridget's thinking – *only* thinking, damn it – that Knostig was poisoned and that's as much as we'll get with the laboratory shut for the weekend.'

'The banks, too.' Lingard was secretly amused by his senior's manifest obliviousness about his involvement with Bridget being known and its effect on his temper. 'It means that we've nothing concrete against Humfries except a petty theft. So far, I'm not latching on to his having clobbered Knostig. Are you intending to have a go at him?'

'Not yet. Let him stew a bit, come to the boil with whatever conscience he has.' Rogers knew how much the silent walls of a cell, a wooden bed and a bolted iron door could be powerful initiators of an inner contemplation of misdeeds done. 'Did you think he was lying?'

'Not so much that as holding back, hiding something fairly disastrous to his future.'

'Knostig could have tackled him about the cheques. If he took them as he says he did, of course.'

'Why not? Although it wouldn't fit in with the matey chin-wagging at the bar. He'd have probably denied having seen him.' Lingard's narrow face showed doubt. 'Would he have given himself up so easily had he killed Knostig?'

'That could be a sort of bluff. Give yourself up for a triviality like theft, make the right kind of stunned noises when you're told that he was dead and who would believe seriously that a murderer would put himself so tamely in our clutches? He'd know he was bound to be picked up sooner or later anyway.'

'You think he might then? Against it too is that actors don't seem to have made much of a mark with murdering people.'

'God knows, and I don't think he's intending telling a mere policeman.'

'I could be wrong,' Lingard said, believing Rogers to be getting over his hung-upness and venturing on lightness, 'but I think he's too amiable a twit, a bit too wet inside. I don't think he could ever nerve himself to do it.'

'Does it need much to dose a man's booze?' He shook his head to negate what he had said. 'No. That would mean pre-knowledge of the meeting and preparation. And whatever it was would probably show or taste in brandy.'

'Exit friend Humfries,' Lingard said without regret, 'except as a fount of information. What about the two females being out at a significant time when he telephoned?'

'That too is only Humfries' version. They could have been out, but they could also have been in. It's a big house and if the phone's downstairs they might not hear it ringing. Or, if they could, to ignore it, suspecting it could only be Humfries making a nuisance of himself.'

'Or that the supposedly missing husband was wanting to know if it was all right for him to come back.'

Rogers had left the window and was pacing up and down, doing his caged lion act. It portended deep thought. 'I've Mrs Knostig very much in mind, David,' he said. 'My problem is that she's so bloody offensive and arrogant that I'm having to fight not to believe her capable of anything. That's prejudice and it has the reverse effect that I'm more inclined to her truthfulness. I can push myself to seeing her feeding him a dose, but can you imagine her lugging him around a churchyard in the dark?'

'Why not?' Lingard was amused. 'You said she was a big woman and now you're offending against the Sex Discrimination Act in implying that she couldn't.'

'Oh, balls to that. I was thinking of whatever feminine delicacy she must have. She certainly didn't wish to identify him as a corpse. Anyway, Humfries – if he's not lying his head off – said that Knostig was well tanked-up when he saw him. That could have been partly due to the effects of poison. And if he had been poisoned during the evening, how long before it would take effect?'

'I think a toxicologist might say it depends on what poison, how much of it and how permeable was the stomach swallowing it.'

'A brilliant statement of the obvious, David,' Rogers said sarcastically. 'I was hypothesizing, not asking. I'd rather know where he was going when he left the bar.'

'Hush my big mouth,' Lingard murmured, having overestimated his senior's amiability.

'Yes,' Rogers said, 'I haven't finished. Wimbush – and he's another liar – says that Knostig could have been on his way

home at chucking-out time. As it's also in the direction of Saint
Boniface Church we can take our pick. It was also some eight
hours after his lunch of duck pâté and biscuits which we can
apparently forget, for Bridget doesn't believe he died of bacterial poisoning.'

'What about Wimbush? Isn't the funeral business too much
of a coincidence?'

'It obviously is. Knowing about the grave has to mean
something. And him a gardener with handy access to a spade.
It'd be second nature for him to dispose of soil on a flower-bed.'
Rogers had stopped pacing, filling his pipe and frowning in
concentration. 'The burial was probably on the afternoon he
wanted off. And that's a reason he chose not to mention. A
motive?' He blew smoke towards the ceiling already yellowed
from it. 'Knostig telling him not to come any more? Knowing
Wimbush, I'm sure his nasty little mind would lean more to
sticking him in the belly with a garden fork, though even he'd
need more reason than that. But it's still too much of a
coincidence.'

'Modified by the fact that anybody reading the *Post and
Messenger* would also know. Your friend, the Very Reverend
Gathercole, would too.'

Rogers was forced to smile and it was less of an effort than he
had anticipated. The thought of the choleric Gathercole creeping around his churchyard dragging a corpse was ludicrous.
'I'll give him the benefit of his cloth,' he said solemnly. 'I don't
believe he'd do anything more diabolical than take his ten per
cent from the collection boxes.'

'Before we leave Wimbush,' Lingard pushed him, 'have you
thought about him leching after Miss Blandford? Or Mrs
Knostig?'

Rogers returned to his looking out of the window. The sun
was at full blaze again and its brightness cheered him, made
him feel less of profligate. There must be hundreds of others,
he again assured his conscience, and all regarding it as less
than a peccadillo. Perhaps what he had done hadn't been so out-

rageous after all. Nevertheless, he didn't wish to think that it had happened – even in theory – between Helen Blandford and Wimbush.

'I wouldn't quarrel about Mrs Knostig,' he said. 'They'd make a suitable couple. It's a sadness that some women have a compulsion to have it off with hairy uncouth primitives, even though they'd never admit it. A sweaty body can turn them on more easily than a cultured mind.'

'As with Lady Chatterley,' Lingard agreed; 'and a distressing thought for men like myself. Although, admittedly, there must be a corollary that some men have a similar disposition to hairy and uncouth females. Couldn't your penetrating analysis of female lechery apply equally well to Miss Blandford?'

'She would be too fastidious.' And that for Rogers was unarguable fact, though not for Lingard who hadn't met her.

'According to Humfries she inclined to lesbianism,' he said. 'Which isn't the most fastidious of sexual relationships.'

'Even if she were – and we've only a put-down boyfriend's opinion on it – there's no motive in that. It could be only excessive affection.' He didn't like the thought of Helen Blandford misusing her sensuality in lesbianism either. 'She's hardly likely to put Knostig away just to have Mrs Knostig for herself. He wasn't in the running anyway,' he pointed out.

'He had to be murdered for something,' Lingard persisted, 'and he has to be something more than just an unwanted woman-chasing husband. Or would that be enough?'

'Anything's enough if somebody's frustrating you in what you want.' Rogers flapped a hand in irritated impatience. 'I'll be a damned sight happier when I know what he died of.'

Lingard smiled. 'You're not still worried about measles or a double hernia?'

'I'm sticking to a vegetable poison. It's all I've got and it had better be right or I'm likely to find myself supervising uniformed beat patrols.' He was brisk, regarding Lingard's relaxing elegantly in his chair with a growing disapproval. He wanted to get on with things, to make up for the hour or so squandered in Bridget's bed. 'So, we've got to find out what Knostig was doing between the time he left home and his meeting Humfries in the Minster. Go and see the estate agents and his solicitor if you can identify and find him, there are about ten of them in the firm. I'll do the health food shop. Knostig didn't reverse the number for nothing. He obviously wanted it concealed, so it has to mean something.'

With Lingard on his feet, he moved to the door. 'There's a woman somewhere,' he said. 'There has to be. If a man's deprived by his wife it's an arguable presumption of fact that he's getting it from somebody else.'

Lingard said, necessarily to himself, 'And you, my dear fella, are the one who should know.'

19

Because he believed that the health food shop might stay in place in the Market Square for an hour or two longer and that he was getting nowhere with his blundering around in the darkest ignorance of vegetable poisons, Rogers called in at the borough library on his way to it.

Climbing the stairs to the reference section – in doing so his knee joints clicked occasionally which, he had noticed, happened only when his body was fatigued – he was given two dauntingly bulky books which he carried to an unoccupied reading table and settled down to a search of their indices. He came quickly to the conclusion that they were handbooks to subtle murder and too easily available. Bridget had been modest in her naming of native poisonous plants. In addition to those she had given him he found monk's-hood, bryony, bittersweet, foxglove, henbane, lily of the valley and thorn apple; all containing the ingredients for a witch's brew of lingering, sometimes painful, death and making him thankful that he hadn't been born a herbivore.

The plants henbane, deadly nightshade and bittersweet interested him in particular. They each contained an alkaloid atropine and this, he found by much dodging from page to page, caused persisting dilation of the pupils, an abnormality of Knostig's eyes to which he was clinging as a characteristic symptom of whatever had poisoned him. Atropine also affected the nervous system, leading to giddiness, dryness of the mouth and possible vomiting. In a sufficient dosage it promoted restlessness and delirium, and caused a depressant action on the vagus nerve which increased the heart-beat. That, in turn, could lead to a fatal asphyxial failure, a footnote remarking that death might not occur for hours or even days. And that could take it back to anywhere and anyone. If Humfries was wrong in his assessment of drunkenness, that could be Knostig suffering from it in the bar of the Minster.

He collected another book illustrating the British flora and returned to his table, a little disgruntled because it was time for a fix and there was a red-lettered *No Smoking* notice prominently displayed over the bookshelves. An hour had gone in his researching and he needed nicotine to stimulate a brain denied its sleep, and to hell with his lungs which could look after themselves.

Except by name, deadly nightshade was an unfamiliar plant to him, but he noted that it grew on limestone hills and should therefore be found somewhere on the moors. The henbane plant illustrated had not come consciously to his notice before. It looked as though it would taste extremely nasty and was, the text informed him, found in sandy soil, especially near the sea. The nearest salt water being fifty miles away, it seemed to cancel it out. Bittersweet was an alternative name for woody nightshade, which fruited scarlet berries as opposed to those of deadly nightshade which were black. It grew commonly in woods and hedgerows and in untended gardens. If he could rely on his visual memory – and he thought he could for shape and colour – Rogers recalled that it also grew in fair quantity, if not commonly, in Mrs Knostig's indoor gazebo and in the netted structures cared for by Wimbush.

Which, he thought, was all very well should the laboratory confirm that Knostig had died of poisoning and from something containing atropine. He was halfway down the stairs, already lighting up his pipe, when the comatose half of his brain stirred momentarily. Cursing his remissness he returned, asking the librarian for a book on British moths.

He couldn't remember the Latin name of the species of moths tossed at him so superciliously by Mrs Knostig, but he did remember that she had called them hawk-moths. There were seventeen listed in the index and he read through the lot, concentrating on the food-plants of their caterpillars. As distinct from the species that ravaged such harmonious-sounding and non-poisonous plants as lady's bedstraw, wild madder, purple loosestrife and goosegrass, he discovered that the huge yellow and violet caterpillars (he remembered seeing those) of the death's-head hawk-moth were known to feed most frequently on the lethally toxic foliage of the potato, bittersweet and deadly nightshade. 'Iron-gutted,' he muttered to himself. 'They must be.'

That the illustration of the moth showed unmistakably the shape of a skull on its back was, he considered with satisfaction, logically appropriate. And, he recognized with even more satisfaction, the moth was undoubtedly identical to those he had seen in Mrs Knostig's laboratory, live and dead.

20

The small squashed-in *Vegetarian Whole Food Store*, flanked by a chemist's and a newsagent's shop, was a building Rogers would normally walk past without interest. Its window was dressed with Chinese bowls of different mueslis, miniature sacks of strange brightly-coloured beans and jars of saffron honey grouped around a huge sheaf of ripe wheat. The alcoved door was locked and Rogers, peering between taped-on cards advising of yoga and weight-watching classes, smoking clinics and organic gardening lectures into the shadowed interior, could see that it was empty. For a Saturday afternoon with the square thick with shoppers it was unusual.

The curtained windows of the floor above the shop suggested living-quarters and he pressed the unmarked bell-push on the wall at the side of the door. Waiting, assuming when there was no reply that Knostig's concealed telephone number might be in the bathroom, (as he himself usually was when he had an unexpected visitor) or struggling to finish dressing, he repeated at intervals his pressing of the bell-push.

He was about to concede defeat when he saw movement at the far end of the shop. The woman who unbolted and opened the door with a languid slowness surprised him. Were she Knostig's secret love, she was as remote from appearing it as anyone he had visualized. Somewhere in her early forties, he judged, and tall, with a thinness that verged on gawkiness, she wore a plain moss-green dress which fell short on concealing her angular hips and the small pod of her stomach. Her light-brown hair was dull and hung in two thick braids over undersized breasts, her nose long in taut features and her unpainted mouth sad. There were mauve shadows under gentle hazel eyes which could be easily hurt and which, he thought, had recently wept. Gold snake-chains were looped around her long throat and there were charm bracelets on her wrists. Her fingernails were transparently lacquered and she wore no rings. Rogers warmed to her on sight. She was a woman he could like without having to want her undress for him.

'I'm sorry,' she said, not visibly irritated by his persistent ringing, 'I'm closed for the day.'

'No, *I'm* sorry for disturbing you.' He held out his warrant card. 'Detective Superintendent Rogers. May I come in and speak to you?'

'Is there anything wrong?' There was an odd dreaminess about her, a lethargy in getting her words out.

'It's about Mr Knostig,' he said without further explanation.

'So you know?' The dismay showing on her face was followed by resignation. 'Please come in.'

While she rebolted the door in her slow-moving manner, he looked around the shop. Cramped for space, the floor's perimeter held large open sacks of rolled oats, muesli, bright orange split-peas and pallid beans; the shelves filled with plastic bags of dried fruits, shelled nuts, bottles of fruit juices and jars of spices. It all looked very wholesome and smelled of a healthy sort of dust, but nothing, he considered, that would set his steak-orientated digestive juices galloping.

He followed her, noticing that she swayed as she walked and had an air of not being with him, through an equally small office stacked with cardboard boxes and up a flight of dark stairs into a sitting-room. A Great Dane dog lying in a patch of sunlight stood as they entered. Biscuit-coloured with a black muzzle, he was as big as a full-grown lion and he pàdded over to the detective to smell him, his tail signalling that he was amiable enough.

Rogers smiled at the woman and said, 'I hope that he's vegetarian as well.'

She didn't smile back, but said, 'He is, and he's a big softie. Don't worry, he won't attack you.'

The furniture and furnishings were solid Edwardian well-off and, he guessed, handed down in succession from her grandparents. There were fading photographs of frowning whiskered men and flat-bosomed women in embossed silver frames on an ornament-crowded mahogany sideboard to support it. Although he could see no anachronistic intrusions such as heating radiators or a television set, there was an array of contemporary bottles of gin, whisky and vermouth on a spindle-legged table. Heavy burgundy-wine curtains hung motionless in the warm currents of air entering the open windows. It was all a little dim and overstuffed, muted and long-piled, but reposeful to the body and mind. He noticed a phantom odour in the room; not of old furniture, of a woman's smell or stale tobacco smoke, but unusual enough to elude him like a short passage of music which, while being familiar, was difficult to identify.

She sat in one of the bloated easy chairs and indicated the other to him. It had obviously been used as a bed by the Great Dane, for his hairs were on its seat cushion. The dog had settled himself at her feet and was watching Rogers with an unwavering stare.

'I know he's dead,' she said unemotionally. 'Had you come to tell me?'

'I'm not sure. I had only your telephone number we found in his pocket.' He was grateful that he hadn't again to go through the breaking of bad news routine. 'I'm sorry, but I don't know your name.'

'Charlotte Inglis.'

'Thank you. *Miss* Inglis?' He was never sure whether Miss or Mrs was the more acceptable guess with a ringless woman in her forties.

'Yes.'

'How did you know that Mr Knostig was dead?'

'I heard it . . . on the local radio this morning. It said the police suspected foul play . . . is that true?' There were pauses in her speaking, as though she were seeking words difficult to find.

'It could be.' Her lack of emotion puzzled him. Had she been Knostig's mistress she should be making at least a token show of distress. Had she not been, he would need to tread very carefully. 'You knew him well?'

'Yes . . . does foul play mean that . . . he was murdered?'

'It might. The circumstances point to it.'

'Would you tell me how?'

'We don't know for certain.' He supposed her need to know

was natural enough, but it was side-tracking his intended questions. 'Please understand, Miss Inglis, that I'm checking on Mr Knostig's movements prior to his death. That was during the night of last Wednesday. And he had visited you recently, hadn't he?' The hairs he had seen on the back of the dead man's blazer and trousers told him that much, and his own clothing was, without a doubt, collecting identical evidence from his chair.

She showed no surprise. 'Yes . . . how did you know?'

He shrugged as if it was of no importance. 'When, Miss Inglis?'

'On Wednesday. It's half-day closing then . . . he called at four o'clock . . .'

'You live here alone?'

'No . . . I have Rufus.' She leaned languidly forward and pinched the skin of the dog's muzzle. 'Why do you ask?'

'Considering the circumstances of Mr Knostig's death,' he said carefully, 'I have to be officially interested in your relationship with him. I hope I'm not embarrassing you?' That had been innocuous enough. Apart from his suspecting otherwise, for all he knew as fact she could be a rabid virgin and litigious to boot. He had only a reversed telephone number to suggest a furtive intimacy, and that would hold no water in a cross-examination by a competent lawyer.

'No, you are not . . . Mr Knostig and I were intending . . . intending to be married,' she said. Seeing his eyebrows rise, she added, 'I know he was already married . . . he never ever kept that from me.'

'Wouldn't a marriage be a little difficult with Mrs Knostig still around?' he asked gently. He could anticipate the lying promises Knostig had made in order to climb into her bed. They were a philandering married man's stock-in-trade for the seduction of morally-inhibited women desperately in need of affection.

'He'd been separated from her for years . . . had already seen his solicitor about a divorce. She was being difficult about the money side . . . he understood that, of course.' Her eyelids were dropping and she pulled a face to keep them open. For a moment, it made her look schoolgirlish. 'When he left me on Wednesday . . . he was going to see her . . . about hurrying it along. I do know that . . . it was necessary.'

He couldn't tell her, he knew. That would be an unnecessary cruelty. Let her keep whatever memories she had of him unbruised for a few days more. 'Was the solicitor with Purves, Dogra and Partners?'

She inclined her head a bare fraction.

'What time did Mr Knostig leave here on Wednesday?'

'About . . . seven to half-past.' Her eyes tried to focus on the old-fashioned chiming clock on the mantelshelf.

'And he was quite all right. His normal self?' Although she was obviously not. Her condition baffled him, for she appeared to be struggling inside herself to stay awake. Although he had not smelled any, he wondered if she had been tipping back anaesthetizing booze.

'I . . . I noticed nothing unusual.'

'Physically, I mean.'

'He was . . . he seemed normal.' She was getting worse with her articulation.

'He had a meal with you?'

'Yes . . . sandwiches and coffee.'

'Would you tell me from the first time you met him? I'm not just being inquisitive and I am discreet. It's important and it may help me to find out who killed him. You would want that?'

'I don't mind your asking,' she said, her words beginning to slur. 'He used . . . used to come into the shop for muesli . . . After a while . . .' Her mouth worked soundlessly for a moment. 'After a while . . . I realized he was buying too much . . . too often for even a large family and . . . and I thought I knew why . . . his manner. He was most pleasant and agreeable . . . then one day when I was having coffee . . . I invited him to join me . . .' She stroked the dog abstractedly, looking away from Rogers as though lost in her thoughts.

'And then?' he asked.

'Yes . . . of course.' Her eyes returned to him and he noticed for the first time how large the pupils were and how expressionless. He read into them an apathy in which nothing really mattered. 'That . . . that was when he told me about his wife . . . that she had walked out and left him. He said he was selling the house . . . he always laughed about how near to bankruptcy he was . . .' Her eyes brimmed with tears, the first sign of emotion she had displayed.

'I'm sorry,' he said, 'I won't keep you much longer.' Her nose was very like his own in shape and that, he had always understood, could indicate a certain bloody-mindedness. If it did, she certainly wasn't showing it.

'No . . . I'm all right. Really I am.' She dabbed at her eyes ineffectually with the back of her hand. 'A month or so ago . . . he said he would be interested in going into partnership in a small business . . . but he had to sell the house first. That would have suited me . . . I am finding it much too much on my own.' A longer pause during which she stared at the dog while Rogers waited patiently. 'After a while . . . then we realized we were fond of each other and . . . and, well, we began to discuss the possibility of marriage . . .'

'And in the meantime he was visiting you regularly?'

'Yes . . . once or twice a week.'

'And leaving always at the same time?' Not a very subtle way, Rogers admitted, of asking her if Knostig ever stayed the night.

'No . . . sometimes later.'

'Late enough to indicate to his wife that he might be seeing somebody else?' The necessary trick question to test her truthfulness.

'How could it . . . they were separated. She doesn't live with him any longer.'

Poor bloody woman, he thought. What lying bastards men could be when they had a frustrated sex life. He said, 'He had something of a problem with his drinking, hadn't he?'

'I'm . . . afraid so.' Her mouth had begun to tremble, a mere twitching, but noticeable. 'He was trying to overcome it . . . I was helping him. But it didn't make any difference to how we felt.'

'He drank too much because he was unhappy? We do, you know.'

'I'm sure he was.' She was now looking as though she were utterly weary and wished to sleep; in a mood of willing compliance to have done with him and hasten his departure. 'But he can't be hurt any more . . . can he?'

'I suppose not.' Rogers believed that to be about the only advantage in being dead. 'Apart from saying he was going to see his wife last Wednesday, was there anything else?'

She let her eyes close as she thought, clearly fighting against her brain shutting down on her. 'Something about seeing bank manager . . . next morning . . .'

'Did he say what for?'

'Cheque . . . I think. Something wrong . . . I can't remember. So many things . . .'

'Did he mention a man called Humfries?'

'No . . . I don't believe so.'

'Can you remember where you were during Wednesday and Thursday nights?' He knew that she wasn't the type to bristle at that.

'I was here . . . where else is there?' There were echoes of years of loneliness in her voice, the vulnerable door through which Knostig must have found it easy to enter.

'Have you a car?'

'Yes . . . I rarely use it though.'

'Have you ever been to Nympton Manor?'

'No. He said . . . people working there . . . knew his wife . . . if I was seen there would affect his divorce.' Her fingers gripped the arms of the chair and she looked at him directly with a heavy-lidded stare. 'You . . . you've noticed that I am pregnant?' Even then there was no bitterness in her voice.

It surprised him, for he hadn't. 'Yes, I had,' he said, not

wanting her to think she had admitted it unnecessarily. 'I'm sorry. It makes things a little awkward, doesn't it?' The understatement of the year, he thought.

'Not . . . not awkward,' she got out, her mouth shaking and her eyelids pink-rimmed. 'Des . . . desolation.'

'He knew?'

'Yes, he had to, hadn't he?' She made him feel that he personified a universal male resentment towards pregnant single women, that he had had a part in her betrayal.

'If there's anything I can do,' he said helplessly and lifted himself from his chair.

He hadn't asked her half enough, but it would be brutal to bludgeon her with insistent questions in the despair he recognized beneath her growing stupor. She had been fighting to conceal it and he had prodded her back into its bleakness. He was about to tell her that he was finished when the identification of the elusive odour he could no longer smell rose to the surface of his mind. The after-traces of cannabis smoking, a recall from the few cases with which he had dealt, although there was no unarguable certainty about it. Nothing he could ever – thank God – prove in a court, but enough to justify his saying things. He should have seen it before. She must be drugged up to the eyeballs, and it explained her mostly dreamlike behaviour in the face of what, for her, must be a calamitous disaster. He had no wish to add to it any more than he had already, but it was imperative that he should know. In his earlier researching he had overlooked that cannabis was also a vegetable poison, that smoking it could cause dilation of the pupils.

She was still sitting, limp and almost completely withdrawn from him, her eyes closed. He looked down at her, certain that something of her mind must still be with him.

'I think you'll understand what I mean, Miss Inglis,' he said gently. 'Did he smoke anything here but his own cigarettes?'

There was a drawn-out silence in which the ticking of the clock was the loudest sound in the room. 'You know?' she whispered at last, not opening her eyes.

'Yes. Did he?' Dammit! He wanted to comfort her in her misery, to somehow numb her grief, and here he was poking more questions at her.

'No . . . never. He didn't know.'

'There'd be no point in concealing it now, would there?'

'No. He didn't . . . he honestly didn't. Only me,' she murmured, so softly that he only just heard it.

'All right, don't let that distress you too.' He placed one of his visiting cards on the arm of the chair and put his hand briefly on her shoulder. 'I'll leave you now and see myself out. If there's anything I can do to help you, anything you want to know, give me a ring.' She was, to all appearances, already gone, the Great Dane licking her lax hand, before he left the room.

Unbolting the door into the late afternoon's sunshine and the pavements crowded with pedestrians unknowing and uncaring of the sadness he had left in the upstairs room, he wondered why he should be so unduly depressed over the sufferings of a woman about whom he knew so little and wasn't too certain that he believed wholly. Even so, he admitted, who did he believe wholly?

Although nothing of what he had learned of Knostig's moral dishonesty made him the less determined to snap handcuffs on his killer, he did prefer his murder victims to appear also to be the victims of cosmic justice. He need not then feel so sorry for their being dead.

21

With Detective Superintendents not being high enough in the Headquarters' hierarchy to be allotted one, Rogers visited the washroom of the absent Assistant Chief Constable and ducked his head in cold water. It helped in clearing the muffling cottonwool inside his skull and he began to feel his thirty-four years again and not a man in his late seventies. He was hungry, too, not having eaten since he had picked half-heartedly at a breakfast that had tasted of the dead Knostig. If he didn't eat soon he would begin to look as herring-gutted as the lean Lingard who, he hoped, was picking up something a lot more useful than he had himself.

He scowled at the swarthy Genghis Khan-like character he imagined he saw in the mirror, a man who could have just returned from cutting the throats of frail and elderly widows. He didn't know what it was to be pregnant, but thought it must be traumatic for a nice gentle spinster of forty-plus, dependent on her own efforts to survive, when the lying fornicating begetter of her unwanted foetus had gone down death's plughole.

Paradoxically, the policeman in him considered that he had been less than zealous in following up the source of the supply of her cannabis. But so be it. He had allowed dangerous compassion to override his zeal and he could be held to have shown partiality. Perhaps he would follow it up when the anguish of her loss had eased. But only perhaps. And that brought the thought that she could have lied protectively about the dead man's involvement in her cannabis smoking. Had he died of an overdose of *Cannabis indica* it would mean an embarrassing end to all his fanciful theorizing.

Returning to his office, he locked the door against any unexpected intrusion by a policewoman – he shuddered at the possible implications – closed the venetian blinds and took off his trousers. Then he removed painstakingly most of the dog hairs from the fabric of the seat and placed them in a cellophane envelope. The laboratory's brains would have to compare the structures of the specimens microscopically before he could accept that the hairs found on Knostig's clothing had come from the Great Dane. Charlotte Inglis might not be the only person known to Knostig who kept a dog, and Rogers was only too well aware how imagined facts could dissipate into non-facts under a later clinical scrutiny. The only thing of which he could be reasonably certain was that the hairs hadn't come from Lockersbie's phantom dog Cerberus.

Retrousered and sitting at his desk, he dialled the number of the hospital and asked to be put through to the Pathology Department. Bridget answered, which indicated that she was there alone. Speaking to him, her voice was warm and possessive and, he thought with exaggerated irony, having an undertone implying that a woman's plaything had come finally to heel. But he accepted that whatever had been morally indefensible about their in-bed conference, it was certainly a catalyst for a female and professional harmony.

'You're lucky to have caught me,' she said after edging him into swearing an almost devoted allegiance. 'I'm only here because I'm doing the report for you. I should have finished earlier had I not been so unexpectedly interrupted.'

He recognized that in her female mind she had already made him the initiator of their coming back together and he accepted it without protest. 'Your postulation about vegetable poisons,' he said. 'I've evidence suggesting it might have been bitter-sweet or deadly nightshade. How do they fit?'

'They could,' she replied. 'I think I mentioned them.'

'So you did. Assuming that I wanted to poison somebody with either and not being able or naïve enough to serve it up as a salad, how would I go about it?'

'Also assuming that whoever did it hadn't access to a complicated distilling apparatus, the same as you'd treat grapes for wine. You'd crush the berries and extract the juice.' She sounded faintly amused. 'If you had a leaning towards *haute cuisine* you could boil up berries, stems and leaves in a saucepan and strain the infusion like tea. The result with either method would be something heavy on atropine and laevo-hyoscyamine instead of tannin. Which, incidentally, is almost as bad for the stomach.'

'And the taste?'

'It might be disguised in anything strong like coffee, neat alcohol or a medicine. It depends how concentrated it is and in what volume it's given. And don't forget, George, physiological tolerance to any poison can make a dose fatal to one person and not to another.'

'What about mixing it with white wine?'

'Yes, if the colouring didn't give it away and whoever was drinking it couldn't tell wine from vinegar.'

'In food?'

'Possible, but not probable. Soups and so on, perhaps.'

'We forgot cannabis, Bridget,' he said as non-committally as he could so as not to suggest that she had been at fault. 'Could Knostig have died from an overdose of it? He was associating with a woman who smokes it.'

'Oh,' she said. 'Let me think.' There was a humming silence while she did so and in it he believed he heard the faint whisper of 'Bugger it', the thump of a book on her desk and the turning of pages.

When she came back to him, she said, 'It just could be, but there are a couple of things against it. I haven't had a case and death from smoking cannabis seems to be unusual. When it does occur it's from a cardiac failure and I found no signs of that, although I wouldn't rule it out completely. It definitely shouldn't result in staining of the stomach lining, although that might be due to a quite separate cause.'

'Like eating too much muesli?' He laughed at his own humour. 'All right,' he said hastily, 'that was supposed to be a joke. Apart from dilated pupils, what are the symptoms of cannabis smoking?' He knew a few of them, but needed a medical confirmation even if she were supplementing it from a text-book.

'In an acute stage of intoxication, vertigo and vomiting . . . a rapid pulse . . . a burning feeling in the throat and chest . . . lack of co-ordination . . . disjointed speech . . . anxiety and restlessness . . . possible hallucinations . . . diminished emotional control . . . you name it and I've a page and a half for you. But,' she added, 'not necessarily all together and obviously not in any moderate usage.'

And that, he told himself – after she had given him the page and a half and elicited from him a promise that he would collect the report personally, and he had replaced the receiver – was all too much of a help.

Despite accepting that once a logical theory had taken lodgement it was illogically difficult to discard, he still couldn't make himself believe that Knostig had died of chronic cannabis – ism, that he himself had been wasting his time thinking on death's-head hawk-moths, bittersweet and atropine. And on the rhinoceros woman. But it did open an already familiar door to nagging doubt and uncertainty. And this uncertainty made him curse the staff of the Forensic Science Laboratory for not sweating at their microscopes over the weekend and thus denying a floundering detective some available and indisputable facts. Knostig's symptoms described by Humfries could, at a pinch, fit what Bridget had told him. Although he was still prepared to believe Charlotte Inglis – well, almost – he had only the word of a hopped-up emotionally disturbed woman to say that her lover hadn't been an addict. Nor need he discount that Knostig wasn't the type to use cannabis because, according to Bridget, it could also increase the pleasure in sexual intercourse and that was indubitably one of Knostig's favourite occupations. Not, Rogers thought piously, an adventitious aberration as it had been with himself and Bridget. Nothing of which helped him to see which way he was going. He reflected derisively that had he been a fictional homosexual Chinese-born university don with *dementia praecox* who condescended occasionally to investigate murders, he would by now have everything tied up to the discomfiture of the floundering detective officer. Or, he added with unusual pessimism, by divining the answer in the entrails of a private eye.

Deciding to eat, he first cleared his IN tray, still conscious that murder took precedence over an empty belly. He scanned quickly through the folder of photographs taken of Knostig's naked body on the necropsy table. One of them, showing the trunk in profile, made him look more closely. Imprinted in the flesh at an acute angle across the chest and stomach were two small circular depressions about six inches apart. They would not have been visible to an eye above them, but had been thrown into shadowed relief by the oblique lighting from the photographer's electronic flash. His feeling was that they were more significant than their ordinariness suggested. They could have been made by buttons, though not by the flat brass discs he had seen on Knostig's blazer. Shirt buttons – he measured the distance between his own with a wooden ruler – were spaced no more than 3½ inches apart and were smaller. It was impossible that trouser buttons – even if they existed – would leave impressions so far above the waist. He was puzzling over their possible origin when the telephone bell rang.

It was the Enquiry Office Sergeant, who told Rogers that a Miss Dorothy Goff was with him, asking to speak to the officer in charge of the enquiry into Mr Knostig's death. It was, he added, apparently important.

Putting the photographs back in the IN tray, Rogers said, 'Send her up' and swore only after he had replaced the receiver. Frowning through the window at the crimson sun dying behind the clutter of rooftops he began to refill his pipe as a substitute for the meal he guessed now he was not going to have.

22

The dumpy woman shown into Rogers's office by a uniformed P.C. walked purposefully to him and held out her hand as he stood. She had a surprisingly firm grip and one, he felt, meant to indicate decisiveness.

'You're Superintendent Rogers?' she said without a smile.

'Yes.' His name and rank being pinned on the outside of the door made that a superfluous question. 'Please sit down, Miss Goff.'

Watching her as she seated herself, he entered into his memory bank the smooth buttery skin about 40 years unwrinkled, deep-blue eyes behind coaster-sized spectacles, thinnish lips painted lightly in mauve and apricot-tinted hair in a well-disciplined bouffant fashion. She wore a lightweight blue tailored jacket and skirt with a paler blue cravat hanging loose and carried a shiny black handbag. She was scentless and wore no jewellery other than a tiny wristwatch and two rings set with aquamarines on the fingers of her left hand. The fingernails were lacquered to match her lipstick. She wasn't fat, but as elegant as plumpness could be with nothing coarse about it. Rogers, who had seen photographs of similar women in the business supplement of his newspaper, considered that she could be irresistible to a man preferring substance to shadow and not minding too much about being treated as a second-class citizen.

'You have something important to tell me about Mr Knostig?' He smiled encouragingly, feeling fairly safe behind his desk.

'My husband,' she said. 'I'm naturally concerned with what happened to him and what you are doing about it.'

It took the smile from his face and he had the feeling that he had been hit from behind with a sand-filled sock. 'You mean Mr Knostig? Richard Francis Knostig?'

'Yes. Didn't you know?'

He stared at her, trying to read things in her face and getting his mind back in order. 'No, I did not,' he said, wanting to swear. 'Nobody thought to tell me, so perhaps you'll be good enough to. He committed bigamy?'

'So far as I know I'm his only legal wife. You thought that woman Tillman was?' It showed in her expression that she wasn't overly impressed with his acumen.

'If you mean Mrs Knostig of Nympton Manor, yes I did. And

you aren't Miss Goff at all, but the real Mrs Knostig?' *You've slipped badly, Rogers, you stupid sod*, he castigated himself.

'I'm both,' she said. 'I use my unmarried name for professional reasons and to avoid embarrassment. That woman living with him is his whore. Her real name is Olivia Tillman and I think she's been married before.'

For God's sake, Rogers marvelled, they're turning up in hordes. How many women had the hyperlecherous Knostig lusted after? By comparison, he himself lived like a cloistered monk, a pallid ascetic.

'Forgive my being dense about all this name-changing and wife-swapping, Miss Goff,' he said, keeping his voice even, 'but suppose you tell me exactly what the current situation is and how it came about.'

'I came here to find out about my husband, Mr Rogers, not to go into my marriage problems.' She wasn't being unfriendly, but rather explaining a simple point to obtuse officialdom.

'And I, Miss Goff,' he said tersely, 'am trying to find out who murdered your husband.' He saw surprise on her face. 'You knew that, didn't you? You must have, so who told you?'

'You did. I guessed that he might have been killed, but not murdered. I was merely told that he was dead and that the police were investigating it.' The news hadn't apparently broken her up. 'How did it happen?'

'Who told you?'

'The Tillman woman. I telephoned this afternoon to speak to Richard and she told me. I think she enjoyed that.'

'It must have been quite a shock.'

'Of course it was,' she said crisply, 'and I've put it behind me. Are you going to tell me what happened?'

'He was, we believe, poisoned; then buried secretly in a local churchyard. We found him last night.'

The surprise in her face had to be genuine. 'Buried!'

'Yes, buried. In an existing grave.'

'My God,' she muttered, her forehead wrinkling. 'How unspeakably macabre. Poor, poor Richard. Did he suffer?' She shook her head. 'No, don't tell me. He wasn't all that bad. Do you know who did it?'

'If you fill in the background of your marriage and Mrs Kn . . . Mrs Tillman's coming into the picture as I asked you,' he said carefully, 'I might be able to tell you – eventually.'

'And then you'll tell me more now?'

'If I can.' He would give her the benefit of any doubt he had that she wasn't weeping her heart out behind her professional woman's façade.

'All right.' She opened her handbag and took out cigarettes, using an enamelled lighter with a hieroglyphic on it and blowing smoke towards the ceiling. 'I've been married to Richard for fifteen years,' she said, looking down at the carpeting at her feet. 'When I met him he was running a butterfly and moth breeding establishment. There's money, you know, in selling native and exotic species to lepidopterists and breeders. That is, if you know what you're doing and stick to it. I worked with him, helped to build it into a very profitable concern. Then . . . don't think I'm being mawkish, but there was a side to it I couldn't stand.' She grimaced. 'Pinned specimens for collectors. Green blood is just as horrible to shed as red. Especially by the hundred and day after day.

'Eventually I refused to do it and tried to persuade Richard to concentrate on live sales only. That didn't work. To give him his due, on the side he did release thousands of the native species to various areas on conservation principles. He had started to drink heavily at the time and had a little trouble with the police. He couldn't drive his car and I hadn't a licence then. All I could usefully do was secretarial work and he already had a girl there who did that and who he wasn't prepared to let go. Money started to become a problem and I got myself a job at Chudlow Airport. Bigger fool me,' she said expressionlessly. 'The next thing I knew was that this Tilman woman had dug herself in from heaven knows where and, apart from doing what I had refused to do, was running the moth side of it as if she owned it. And bringing a grant or something similar with her to do scientific research with them. It suited Richard who preferred anyway to wear a bowler hat and superintend. That was six years ago and she wasn't quite so haggish then. At least, Richard didn't seem to think so.' She lifted her head and looked at him. 'Why am I telling you all this?' she demanded.

'Because you're helping the police with their enquiries,' he said, thinking that she was softer inside than she was allowing him to see. 'Putting a bit of flesh on old skeletons. You really can help me.'

She mashed her cigarette carefully on the ashtray he pushed over to her and returned to looking at the patch of carpeting. 'When I realized that Richard was jumping into bed with her as soon as my back was turned, I left them to it. With dam' all in fact, although I've made it since.'

'And you changed your name.'

'No. I reverted to my own name. I saw a solicitor and it's quite permissible and legal. That was no problem.'

'None also for Mrs Tillman to change to Knostig, although it sounds unnecessarily conformist to me. Why would she do that?'

'Why not ask her? Who knows what was in her nasty little mind? She was living there for a start. Not that it's done her any good.' There was gritty spite in her words. 'Richard wanted to get rid of her and sell the house.'

'He told you this?'

'Yes. So far as he and I were concerned it's all been quite civilized. He's weak, you know, not wicked, and I never lost all the affection I had for him.'

'Neither of you wished for a divorce?'

'It may sound commercially-minded to you, but for a woman a husband is money in the bank and security. You don't give that away to a scheming whore. Particularly not when you don't intend to remarry. So far as he was concerned, yes, he did ask for a divorce earlier on but soon changed his mind. Poor man,' she said sadly, 'he's got it now, if not quite the way he'd have wanted it. He was anxious that I should go back to him when he'd got rid of her and I was thinking seriously about it because the lease on my flat runs out next year. And because returning would have the effect of stopping him from selling Nympton Manor.'

So would being killed, Rogers reminded himself. It was beyond his understanding that a woman should wish to return to a marriage which had caused her enough humiliation for her to have abandoned it. She had been too submissive about it considering her fighting weight. In her shoes, before leaving, he would have torn the supplanter's hair out and thrown her down the steps. It wouldn't have been very ladylike, but satisfying and making any future return less of a surrender.

'I'm surprised you were on speaking terms,' he said, comparing it with his own folded marriage. 'I thought that separated husbands and wives always had their canines bared for the jugular vein. I take it he used to visit you and not the other way around?'

'Yes, and I see nothing to be surprised about. We weren't proposing to . . . well, it would have been a matter of convenience for both of us. Financially and housewise.'

'When did he last visit you?'

'Last Wednesday. He came about eight o'clock.'

'A routine visit?' He wanted to ask if they'd finished up in bed, but his professional curiosity couldn't be stretched that far. Perhaps they hadn't. He had noticed that her ample breasts were well battened down which, together with the non-wearing of a predatory scent, might suggest a certain withdrawal from active sex. He could be mistaken, but he thought that sleeping with her might be like snuggling up to a metal filing cabinet.

'There were no routine visits,' she said. 'He'd telephoned to tell me he would be coming to discuss what we were going to do and what he was going to do about that woman.'

'And you did?'

'Of course. He was returning that night to tell her that he was going on with the selling of the house – which he agreed wouldn't exactly be the truth – and that she'd have to go. He was quite determined about it.'

Which of them, he wondered, had been told the truth; she or Charlotte Inglis? Probably neither. Knostig should have taken up a career of fraud by false pretences. 'Together with Miss Blandford?' he asked.

'Oh, her. She's not important. She's a paid assistant.'

'You know her?'

'I've never met her, nor do I particularly wish to. Richard told me about her. She was throwing herself at him and it made things awkward for him there.'

'I'd be surprised if that were the case,' he said shortly. 'What time did your husband leave you?'

She frowned, taking another cigarette and lighting it. 'I'm not sure. He was with me for at least an hour, possibly more. Why do you ask?'

'So far as we know, he died that night.'

Her eyes widened and her mouth made a small O, smoke curling from it. 'You mean . . . after he left me?'

'Much later. What was he like . . .'

The telephone bell interrupted him and he said 'Excuse me', lifting the receiver and answering it. He heard a click and then only the hissing of static until the switchboard operator came in. 'Sorry, sir,' he said, 'she cut herself off.'

'Who's she?'

'A lady, sir. She wouldn't give her name, just said you'd know her and that it was very important.'

'If it is she'll ring again.' He replaced the receiver thoughtfully, returning his attention to Miss Goff. 'I was about to ask you,' he said, 'what was he like when he was with you?'

She pursed her lips and frowned. 'As always, I suppose. No, now I come to think about it, he wasn't. He was on edge, jumpy. I remember now, he did say that he had a headache although he wouldn't take the paracetamols I offered him. He'd been drinking and I don't blame him with having to put up with that bitch. Anyway, not so much that he was about to fall flat on his face.'

136

'Nothing else? His eyes, for instance.'

She looked puzzled. 'His eyes? I don't know what you mean.' When he didn't explain, she said, 'I think he was worried about something.'

'He didn't say what?'

She shook her head. 'No, and he'd have told me had it concerned us.'

'You gave him a meal? A drink?'

'I gave him nothing and he wanted nothing,' she said flatly with a brief show of annoyance. He was beginning to irritate her. 'I don't drink myself and I don't keep it in the flat.'

'Do you keep a dog?'

She gave him a darkly suspicious glance. 'In a flat? No, I don't keep a dog, or a cat either. Why would you want to know that? Why all the questions?'

He showed his teeth disarmingly, seeing angry words looming. As with the other Mrs Knostig, he didn't believe that she was developing much of an affection for him. That was fair enough, she hadn't come to him to be cross-examined.

'Just questions, Miss Goff. Polite ones. Bear with me, please. Does the name Charlotte Inglis mean anything to you?'

She bit her lip at that and looked hurt. It left a thin line of mauve on her teeth. 'I see. There's another woman.' She was silent for a few moments, thinking about it. 'Who is she?' she asked, her voice peremptory.

'You don't know her, then?'

'No, and I want to know who she is.'

'Unfair as it may seem, I can't discuss her with you. No more than I could discuss with her what you have told me.'

'I see. Does it mean that Richard was lying to me?' She was shrewd with her counter-questions and keeping him a degree off balance.

'If he was – and I don't know – it doesn't matter now.'

'It does to me,' she said sharply. 'I don't like being taken for a fool. Was he serious about her?'

Rogers disliked being the destroyer of images as he so often had to be and he equivocated. 'Probably not. Don't make too much of it. What were you telephoning him about this afternoon?'

Her eyes behind the large spectacles narrowed as she stared at him. 'He promised faithfully that he'd tell me what happened when he'd spoken to that woman. When he didn't . . . well, that was over three days ago.'

'So?'

'So I telephoned to find out.'

'And Mrs Knostig . . . I'm sorry, Tillman, answered. What did she say?'

'I asked to speak to Richard and she said, "Haven't you heard?" I said, "Heard what?" "He's dead," she told me. Just like that, God rot her soul.' Rogers could hear the underlying bitterness. 'I said, "What do you mean?" I was terribly shocked. Then she said, "I mean just that. If you wish to know anything further you'd better speak to the police. They are investigating it." Then she put the phone down on me.'

'And that was it?' He had a mental picture of the two women expending their hatred over a dead man's corpse that neither had wanted when it was breathing.

'Not entirely. When I'd got over the shock I telephoned again. I was prepared to be very angry and I think she realized how distressed I was. At least, she seemed more sympathetic. She told me that Richard had been missing and that he'd been found dead, that the police wouldn't tell her how he'd died but it was obviously under suspicious circumstances. She said she couldn't talk about it because she was upset herself and knew nothing about it anyway. I think she's a liar,' she said calmly.

'We can all lie under stress,' he said ambiguously.

'She's got to get out. It's mine now.'

'You mean the house?'

'Of course I mean the house.'

'You'll have to get legal advice on that. She might be regarded as a sitting tenant.'

She compressed her lips and said, 'The bloody bitch.'

'It's an opinion,' he said, 'and I advise you strongly not to have any further contact with her. Certainly not while this investigation is in progress.'

'I shall think about it.' She hadn't liked being told.

He had come to the hard part again. The part where those he questioned bristled, burst into flames or lied with an utter sincerity. 'I have to ask you this,' he said as if it didn't matter one way or the other. 'Will you account for your whereabouts during the nights of Wednesday, Thursday and Friday?'

She was one of those who bristled and she frowned, her eyes probing his. 'Do you realize what you are implying?'

'I'm not implying anything,' he said wearily. 'I ask everybody. I'm almost tempted to ask myself sometimes. I have to do reports. Reports are supposed to cover every aspect of an investigation. And that includes the who, when, where and why of everybody, however remotely connected. You're satisfied?' he asked, watching the frown weaken.

Why were people so bloody sensitive about this, he wondered, and then – OK, so where were *you*, Rogers, and a certain female pathologist between the hours of one and three o'clock, and don't burst a blood vessel over an innocent question. The plump Miss Goff might, although improbably, have been occupied by being climbed over in bed by a hardy lover.

'Not wholly,' she replied, 'but I'll tell you. I was working at the airport.'

'The *nights*, Miss Goff.'

'That's what I'm telling you. I'm the Deputy Controller Night Staff of the Data Communications, Management and Planning. Other than Sundays, I'm on duty from ten to six o'clock each night. Does that cover whatever's in your mind?'

'I've nothing in my mind,' he said, believing it almost literally true. He had the odd feeling that he was all face with nothing much behind it. 'You have a car?'

'I didn't walk here. Nor do I walk to the airport.'

'May I have your address, please, in case I need to see you again?'

She opened her handbag and handed him a card. 'Is there anything else?'

'Would you be prepared to identify your husband for the Coroner?'

She hesitated. 'If I have to. Yes, of course.'

'I'll arrange a time convenient for you.' He rose and moved from behind his desk. 'I'll see you out,' he said. She had apparently forgotten her demand for more details of her husband's death and he wasn't going to remind her, deciding that he was frail flesh and tired mind and had, for the moment, had a surfeit of asking awkward questions and getting contradictory answers. And not getting far with them either.

It did enter his mind whether a dark-blue uniform and a silver-peaked cap might not reflect his professionalism rather better than the grey worsted suit he now wore to such little effect.

23

Back at his desk, Rogers stared glumly into the charred bowl of his empty pipe, wondering whether he could afford to refill it so soon. Weeks ago in an idle few seconds he had worked out on his pocket calculator the cost of the tobacco he used. In happy ignorance he had been paying an outrageous £46,000 a ton for it; more shatteringly, well over 85,000 American dollars. He considered it a high price to pay for blackened lungs as he stuffed more of the precious stuff into his pipe. It reflected his mood.

It might have been because his brain cells were starved of sleep that he felt unwontedly pessimistic about maintaining his so far 100-per-cent successful murder investigation record. There would come a time when he would fail and he accepted this as a statistical certainty. But with each new case he would

pray *Not this one, dear Lord. Not this one.* Although he believed it to
be a transitory pessimism, even that was no comfort. Nothing in
this case, he thought, was anything but unsubstantiated sur-
mise and suspicion. The only concrete fact he had was that
Knostig was dead. Or a man was dead whom he had to assume
was Knostig, for nobody to whom he was known had yet
identified him. Nor did he know from what he had died;
whether, for certain, he had been murdered, had committed
suicide or died accidentally from a lethal intake of cannabis
smoke. And no chemist or toxicologist from the laboratory was
going to tell him for unwaitable days. Could he see any profit
from it, his frustration would easily provoke him into hurling
his telephone handset through the window glass into the
growing darkness of the street.

He read again the table of events and non-events he had
written out in the unlikely hope that it might stir into life
something akin to a divine revelation.

Wednesday:	*2.00 p.m. Knostig leaves Nympton Manor.*
	4.00 p.m. Knostig visits Charlotte Inglis until 7–7.30 p.m.
	8.00 p.m. Knostig visits Dorothy Goff until 9.00 p.m. plus.
	10.00 p.m. Knostig at Minster Hotel with Humfries.
	10.30 p.m. plus. Citroën Safari seen by Wimbush entering Market Square.
Thursday:	*3.00–8.00 a.m. Estimated time of Knostig's death.*
	Midnight. Humfries in Spye Green, adjacent Nympton Manor.
Friday:	*1.00 a.m. Lockersbie finds Knostig's body in church porch.*
	2.40 a.m. P.C. Wates sees Citroën Safari being driven towards railway station.
	5.10 a.m. Lockersbie reports finding of body to Station Sergeant.
	6.00 a.m. D./Sgt Simpson visits church and finds body removed.
	8.00 a.m. Olivia Knostig reports Knostig missing.

4.30 p.m. Citroën Safari found in station car park.
3.00 a.m. Knostig's body found by D./P.C. Brooker.
5.30 a.m. Preliminary examination at mortuary by Dr
Hunter – time elapsed since death 45–50 hours.

There was no divine revelation. It told him nothing he did not already know, or anything from which he had not already drawn conclusions. And conclusions made without provable facts to support them were lurking dangers for a policeman whose career and bank balance could be damaged in an action for an unlawful arrest and detention. Plunging around like an impulsive bonehead with handcuffs at the ready had never been Rogers's way.

There were gaps in the table which, when filled, should provide useful answers. One was the two hours between Knostig's leaving home and calling on his pregnant mistress, another hour at least after leaving his lawful wife and meeting Humfries. A wider gap was that between his being seen (if he was) by Wimbush in the Citroën and his dying. Following that, the several hours during which he had been lying dead on his stomach on a hard surface – and where the hell could that have been? – before being taken to Saint Boniface's Church for secret burial. All subject, of course, to everybody concerned having told the unvarnished truth – which, Rogers knew, was as unlikely as it would be surprising.

Before leaving the office, he telephoned and spoke to the Chief Security Officer at Chudlow Airport. Within minutes he had called back to confirm that Miss Goff had, indeed, been on duty on each of the nights Rogers had asked about and, no, there was positively no possibility that she could have left her office during her tours of duty. Which, Rogers thought, only underlined how straw-clutching he was becoming, how paranoiac about everybody, no matter how improbably connected with Knostig's death.

'To man who has manure on boots,' he growled to himself, 'the whole world smells of manure.'

24

Rogers braked his car to a halt between the open gates of Nympton Manor when he saw in the beams of his headlights a small white car parked on the gravel forecourt. He recognized it, having seen it being driven away from Police Headquarters only an hour or so previously. The bloody woman had deliberately disregarded his advice. Reversing, he drove a few yards along the road into the shadow of a tree and switched off the lights.

Locking the doors – he could think of no more embarrassing happening than a policeman's car being stolen – he entered the gates and walked on the grass at the side of the drive towards the house. The heat of the day was still in the soil, the warm odours of damp vegetation rising to his nostrils.

The moon, full-flooding a sky in which the stars were dimmed by its luminescence, in which small flocculent clouds glided, painted the night with a clear lividity. Two oblongs of orange light shone from ground-floor windows in the gleaming façades of the building.

He looked into the white car and then put his hand on its bonnet, feeling it tepid. It had been there a longish time. She had possibly gone directly from him to 'that scheming whore' as she had so contemptuously called her.

He climbed the steps to the door, his fingers hesitating on the brass knocker as the sounds of raised voices came to him from inside. Unintelligible and unrecognizable behind the solid wood, they were clearly the hard angry words of women with their talons unsheathed, nothing in them of well-bred coolness. But more civilized, if more wounding, he supposed, than male fists.

Taking his fingers from the knocker he retreated down the steps, accepting that this might be no occasion for a show of his official presence. He would postpone his further questioning and that which he wished to do in addition could be done better without a necessarily ambiguous explanation.

With the moon temporarily clouded, he walked noiselessly between the dark bushes to the netted cage in which he had interviewed Wimbush. The door bolt was unoiled and squeaked loudly when he slid it back. Inside, he used his pocket torch, shining its discreetly narrow pencil of light along the rows of plants. Small moths and flies rose and flew in its beam. When he found and recognized the ovate leaves and red berries he was looking for he broke off two small sprays and put them in the cellophane envelope he had brought with him. Because there was never any certainty in speculation, he searched for the spade he had seen earlier. A specimen of the soil from its blade could be characteristic and identifiable to a location. It had been removed, together with the fork he had seen with it.

Bolting the flimsy door behind him, he strode past the dark mass of the tool shed towards the gates, pausing when he heard a spasmodic grunting. A wandering hedgehog hunting slugs was his first thought, except that it appeared to be coming from inside the shed. His second was that Wimbush was pig-snoring in what Helen Blandford had told him was his occasional bed. If he was, Rogers considered it unusual that he had not heard him unbolting the cage door.

He retraced his steps to the door and listened, hearing a soft whimpering, a counterpoint of sound to the animal grunting. Looking through the small window at its side into the deeply-shadowed interior, straining to focus on indistinct shapes, he made out at floor level a pallid roundness that rose and fell with a metronomic rhythm. As he watched, realization growing in his mind, the moon emerged from behind the cloud, illuminating the squat bulk of Wimbush, his cap on, his trousers down around his thighs and exposing buttocks that beat at the woman flattened beneath him. Two slim legs on either side of his, a pulled-up rumpled dress and the pale oval of Helen Blandford's face turned sideways, her eyes closed and the whimpering coming from her parted lips.

As the shaken Rogers turned away from his unintentional voyeurism, her eyes opened and she looked directly up at him. He couldn't know whether she had recognized him or had glimpsed only his dark silhouette, but one or the other she had and he swore vilely. Shivering as if with the ague, he was seized by an unfamiliar barbarity of emotions erupting through his grey-suited professionalism. He fought the atavistic compulsion in him to bare his teeth and yell, to tear the shed apart slat by slat, to burst in and beat the gross and brutish Wimbush to a bloody pulp.

It had been past his imagining how any woman so elegant, of such delicate sensibilities, so physically refined, could give herself to a sweaty and ignorant lout such as Wimbush. What she was doing was an affront to his uncharacteristic belief in cultured feminine fastidiousness.

Standing in the shadow of a bush away from the hut, he forced himself to wait – when he needed to put distance between him and them – and to rationalize his Detective Superintendent persona back into dominance. What the hell was it to do with him anyway with what coarse lecher she satisfied her body? And that, he admitted, was what he himself had wanted and, because he was what he was, could not. For that brief moment of realization, though believing himself anaesthetized by Bridget against Helen Blandford's sensuality, he had allowed his goat-legged *alter ego* to take over. She should be, damn her, only a bloodless cipher in an impersonal investigation and what she and Wimbush were doing no more than a factor to be considered in it. He had succumbed like a spotty teenager to sexual jealousy in its worst form and, recognizing that crestfallen genitalia were but an illusory humiliation, managed to smile wryly in the darkness. He wasn't quite back to being happy, but he was no longer anguished either. He should have gone into the shed and parodied the traditional, ''Ello, 'ello,

'ello. What's goin' on in 'ere then?' Self-derision, the great anodyne, and he thought he might now live without worms chewing holes in his subconscious.

She came from the shed within minutes, a flitting wraith of a woman in the shadowed moonlight, her face not visible to him and walking swiftly over the grass without looking around her. Passing the parked car, she went to the side of the house and out of his sight. The door of the shed remained closed.

When a light came on in one of the upstairs windows, he threaded his way between the bushes to stand under a tree in the shadow of the perimeter wall to await the departure of Dorothy Goff. Turning to face the house he sensed movement behind him, heard the light rustle of trodden-on grass. He was too late in reacting to it: an arm whipped hard around his throat and strangled his involuntary shout. Simultaneously, a hand clamped on his wrist, forcing his arm painfully up between his shoulder-blades. With his free arm bent and poised to drive his elbow backwards into his attacker's stomach, he smelled the perfume of Attar of Roses. 'You bloody fool, David,' he croaked. 'For Christ's sake, you're breaking my neck!'

If there could be disappointment felt in the relaxing and withdrawing of pinioning arms, it was there. 'Sorry, George.' Lingard, releasing him and stepping back, was a denser shape in the blackness of the wall as the ruffled Rogers turned to face him. 'I thought you were a villain up to no good and I wasn't intending to lose two in one day.' His teeth glimmered in a smile.

'You nearly lost your dinner,' Rogers growled, straightening his crumpled shirt collar and dislodged tie. 'I thought you were Wimbush. And keep your voice down, he's over there in the shed. What are you doing here anyway?'

'Apart from seeing a villainous character creeping around private property with a torch, I've been checking on friend Humfries' visit up here. A lover's view from a telephone kiosk. It'd be good if there were not a tree or two blocking it.'

'You mean he couldn't see the house?' They stood shoulder

to shoulder now, watching as they talked, although Lingard would probably not know what.

'Not at night. It's barely possible to see a lighted window through the leaves, improbable that he could have identified the location of a room.'

'He needs jumping on.' Nevertheless, Rogers wasn't anxious for Humfries to be involved in Knostig's murder. Anything implicating him would undermine the little evidence he had pointing to who had done it, make more confusing the uncertainty about how it possibly could have been.

'I jumped on him this afternoon,' Lingard said cheerfully, 'and from a great height. A lot of held-back anguishing about should he or should he not come clean about the cheques. Then bottling up to think some more about it because I hadn't anything new to chuck at him. No bank manager available, of course – he's gone to the coast for the weekend. No estate agents open either. But I saw the house advertised in Mayhew Brothers' window. Would you give £69,999 for it?'

'Not until it'd been painted and the lawns mown. A wasted effort, David. That hasn't been in doubt since I spoke to Knostig's girlfriend this afternoon and to his one and only lawful spouse this evening. She's the one whose car we're watching.' He gave Lingard the bones of his interview with the two women.

'What's she doing up here?' Lingard asked.

'Trying to convince Mrs Knostig Number Two that she has to vacate the house, I imagine. I heard female voices screeching at each other from outside.'

'And you went and hid in the cage with your torch?'

'Grabbing a couple of specimens of bittersweet, David. *Solanum dulcamara*, if you had to research on it as I had. I'm almost certain it's the stuff that killed Knostig. If it wasn't cannabis or something else altogether,' he said, minimizing his certainty as an insurance against being found wrong.

'Grown by Wimbush. Is that why you thought it was him trying to throttle you? Because you pinched some of his plant?'

Rogers rarely kept anything from his second-in-command, who had not, he guessed, seen Helen Blandford leave the shed. He had no wish to pass judgement on the woman whose fastidiousness he had so confidently defended to Lingard. Now that his blood had stopped running hot and he was thinking with his mind and not with his loins, he could see implications. In his brief glimpse of her she had appeared flaccid and non-responsive, with no show of passion and seeming not to be enjoying Wimbush's ministrations. And she had told him that she didn't like him – for what it was worth. It all needed thinking about on his own.

'I knew he was in the shed,' he said, 'and he could have heard me, come to the same conclusion that you did.' He felt his throat. 'Perhaps not quite so roughly.' He steered the talk away from Wimbush. 'I know you don't wear them, David, but would you agree you'd take your spectacles off to go to bed?'

'I've always thought so. You're on to something?'

'I might be. Would you also take them off to make love? In bed, I mean.'

'A loaded question, George,' Lingard said, poker-faced. 'My grandfather had a bespectacled girlfriend and I know for a fact that she always took hers off. There's always the risk of severe slashing in the ensuing mêlée.'

'He told you, I suppose?' Rogers smiled, for he guessed that Lingard had been his own grandfather. 'Without suggesting that you have one, would you take your pyjamas with you when visiting a mistress?'

'Not unless I wanted to lose her. It'd be a mite Victorian, wouldn't it? Like doing it with your hat and overcoat on.'

'I wouldn't either, but Knostig might were he deferring to a prim and proper mistress.'

'Good Lord!' Lingard was amused. 'Are there any?'

The light in the upstairs window had gone out and, in the silver rectangle of reflected moonlight, Rogers thought he could see a shadow of movement that remained there long moments as they talked. It had to be Helen Blandford and he forbore mentioning it. Lingard could see and draw his own conclusions, ask if he couldn't. 'So where do you wear pyjamas other than in your own bed or with an uptight girlfriend?'

'In hotels?'

'Yes, but you wouldn't be left lying around dead for the best part of a night and day. And probably on the floor.'

'And you think Knostig was?'

'It's the only place I can think of. There are depressions in his belly which could have been made by pyjama buttons. There's no proving it, of course, but if they are then he was dressed again after he died.'

'Then it could have happened here. Which one? Or don't I work with you any more?' Lingard said it lightly, but Rogers accepted that he might feel a little put out.

'I'm not keeping anything I *know* from you, David,' he said. 'If I knew, if I had any evidence, if I were even half sure, I'd tell you and be acting on it.'

'It seems pretty clear to me, George. Knostig comes back home full of booze and nastiness, has a flaming row with Mrs Whatsername who slips him a Micky Finn and he goes off to bed, gets out of it when he feels the first pangs and dies on the floor. She waits until the next night, dresses him, takes him to the churchyard and buries him. The following morning she reports him missing, but by the grace of Saint Boniface, poor old Lockersbie and a hungry fox, all is discovered.'

'And that's what you call being pretty clear,' Rogers said drily. 'I agree the general synopsis, but it doesn't fit by half.'

'I'm guessing,' Lingard murmured, 'and as baffled as you appear to be.'

The door opened in the front of the house to a momentary yellow illumination and Dorothy Goff stumped down the steps into the moonlight. Even in that, anger was visible in her face and her slamming of the car's door emphasized it.

When she had driven through the gates in a scattering of gravel, Rogers checked his wristwatch. 'Nearly nine o'clock,' he said yawning, 'and I'll think about it tomorrow. We're knocking off for the night before we drop unconscious.' He gave Lingard a good-humoured scowl, wanting no more questions. 'Remind me in the morning to have you charged with an aggravated assault on a senior officer. It should help your promotion prospects considerably.'

25

Rogers's home had reverted to being a house, a brick shell in which to sleep and occasionally to eat; to use as an address for his mail and somewhere to garage his car. It was empty of another's occupancy and echoed a deserted marriage in its silence. At times he had even wished it haunted; preferably, he qualified, by something female, reasonably young and attractive and not given to groaning him awake on the too few occasions he got into bed before midnight.

This was an early night to return to it, for he had spent only a further hour at his desk after dismissing Lingard to his own bed. He had sent for P.C. Wates and persuaded his recall back to the night when he had seen the Citroën Safari being driven at 2.40 a.m. towards the railway station. Could he remember, he asked him, if the Citroën had been the only vehicle in the street at that ungodly hour? Wates had thought about it and then given Rogers the answer he had hoped for. There had been one other car following close behind the Citroën. He was unable to recall its description and suggested that this was because it had probably looked like any other standard model, where the Citroën had not. It was more than Rogers had expected and for a few seconds his world had been a euphoria of conscientious and alert-brained night-duty constables.

Soggily tired and mentally fatigued, certain that his body fluids had drained out through the soles of his feet, he drank a very large undiluted whisky. Then he blundered ineptly about his kitchen percolating coffee and grilling a pork chop which, carelessly charred, he decided he couldn't stomach. Putting it in the refrigerator, optimistic that he could eat it for his breakfast, he drowned the whisky with two cups of coffee, black and bitter because the milk left on the doorstep all day had turned sour. Too weary to smoke a final pipe of tobacco, he stumbled up the stairs like a drunken man.

He was often subjected to vivid nightmarish dreams when overtired, and the whisky, intended as immunization against them, failed. Mrs Knostig, mad-eyed and leather-plated like a rhinoceros, hunted him across a twilit landscape of shadowed valleys and, following at her heels, a gliding figure with the body of Helen Blandford and the fiercely grimacing features of Wimbush. Sombre moths as big as sparrows and black butterflies like bats swarmed above and harried him with sharp snapping teeth as he fled.

His comatose mind accepted these grotesque simulations of his subjective assessments as phantasmagoria signifying nothing more than any other dream. But that which followed, the re-enactment of an actual solitary happening, woke him shouting a horror that until now his brain had repressed.

Pyjama-less, shuddering and only half-awake, he felt his way downstairs in the dark and drank more whisky to numb the unwelcome recall before returning to a dreamless sleep.

When the telephone bell brought him up from the depths of his unconsciousness there were long moments before his blindly groping hand found the receiver and he was able to grunt into it.

'Chief Inspector Denham here, sir,' he heard in the far reaches of his sleep-drugged brain. 'I've been informed by the hospital that they've a patient there who's suffering from the effects of a poison. She's a Miss Dorothy Goff and apparently she's recovered enough to ask that you be told.'

When he had said vile things he could not remember a few minutes later and replaced the receiver, he switched on the light. It was five-thirty, still dark outside and unbelievable that he had had a full six hours of supposedly refreshing, rejuvenating sleep. Too many of his brain cells must have died in the night and he was surprised when he looked into the bathroom mirror that he hadn't grown a septuagenarian's grey whiskers to go with the bloodhound-sad eyes that couldn't possibly belong to him.

26

Even when mentally tranquil and in prime breeding condition with no aches, pains or bleeding holes in him, Rogers disliked the hospital for its atmosphere of suffering. Entering it in the grey light of dawn to the smells and sounds of ordeal and anguish being awakened to face another day was as much a reminder of his own mortality as would have been the reading of his newspaper over the breakfast he hadn't had. Perhaps, he comforted himself, it would never happen to a much older Rogers, who would do his damnedest to die outside it and standing up.

The Dame Janet Woodbridge Ward was already illuminated for the coming day with all its beds occupied, the faces in them turned towards him with all the disquiet of believing him a visiting funeral director. He knocked on the door of the Ward Sister's office and entered.

He knew Sister Anderson as he knew most of the hospital staff. There existed a working affinity between nurses and policemen, extending to those nurses not marrying into the medical profession more often than not making do with policemen.

'I'm looking for the doctor, Morag,' he said, 'and you're looking extremely attractive this morning.'

As indeed she was; tall and slim, black-haired and Welshaccented, she wore the navy-blue uniform and linen cap her feminine competence with the sick and dying had earned. 'I love you too, George, even though you haven't bothered to shave.' She stood up from her desk, looking at the fob watch pinned over her bosom. 'You're late, and Dr Mukherjee is attending a call at the moment. You're here to see Miss Goff?'

He grinned. 'I haven't come to a females' ward for treatment,' he said. 'Not yet. Can you tell me what happened?'

'That's what I'm here for. And put your pipe away. You know you can't smoke in here.' She picked up a sheet of paper from her desk and referred to it. 'She was admitted to Casualty at 1.40 a.m. in a state of collapse, but still conscious. Examination by Dr Warwick and the symptoms recorded as raised temperature, rapid pulse, skin flushed and dry and partially dilated pupils. The patient complained of gastro-intestinal irritation and extreme thirst. Questioned about what she had eaten, she said she believed she had been given poison in a drink, would not or could not say by whom nor what it could be. She was given a stomach wash and catheterized against urine retention, after which she was admitted to this ward for observation.'

'And she asked that I should be told.'

'Yes, when she'd recovered – more or less.' Her brown eyes were bright and clear for someone who had been up all night and Rogers was not so tired that he couldn't wonder if she was still married and unobtainable.

'I can see her?'

'She's not going to die, George. At least, Dr Mukherjee doesn't think so.' That, to Rogers, didn't represent certainty, but he accepted it.

'What does he believe poisoned her?'

'He doesn't. He guesses one of the mydriatic alkaloids, but unfortunately Dr Warwick didn't take specimens of the stomach wash or urine.'

That, Rogers thought, would be bloody useful in prosecuting a case of poisoning and it fitted in well with the frustrations of the investigation. It must have shown in his expression for she said, 'He's a first-year man, George, and doesn't have the deplorable mind of a detective.'

'It doesn't matter,' he lied, smiling at her friendly insult. 'Do you know the circumstances of her being brought here?'

'Only at about third hand. She apparently vomited, then collapsed or fainted at the airport and whoever it was with her called for an ambulance.' She moved towards the door. 'She's been ordered complete rest and quiet so you'd better be quick. I'll give you ten minutes.'

He followed her crisply rustling figure through the ward to the small room at its end. Isolated in a small cone of light from a wall lamp, the plump woman opened her eyes as they entered. Rogers was always in two minds whether to smile cheerfully at the hospitalized and appear unsympathetic, or to be solemn and look as though he were visiting before it was too late. Doing neither, he nodded without expression.

When Sister Anderson had departed after feeling Miss Goff's pulse and rearranging her pillows, he sat on the chair at the side of the bed. The smart elegance that had been the professional woman's persona in his office was no longer there. Her hair was drab and straggling, her mouth colourless, her pale face looking fat and matronly in the absence of her spectacles. Paradoxically, despite her plumpness, she looked frail. She wore a white shroud-like hospital nightdress and was manifestly unhappy. It made him feel less conscious of his unshaven jowls and chin.

'I'm sorry about this,' he said. 'Are you well enough to tell me what happened?'

She glanced at him without turning her head and it made her look frightened. 'They won't tell me,' she whispered. 'Am I going to die?'

He smiled then, exuding confident assurance. 'Good Lord, no. They wouldn't have let me in here if you were.'

'You're not just saying it?'

'You're probably feeling like the end of the world, but you're not within miles of it.'

She rolled her eyes at him; no longer dilated, he noticed. 'You're not a doctor, though.'

'Miss Goff,' he said patiently, knowing his ten minutes were going fast. 'When a person from whom we wish material information about a crime is dangerously ill and dying, we arrange for a justice of the peace to be present to take a deposition on oath. As there isn't one here, you are obviously not dangerously ill and dying.'

'I feel dreadful,' she said, more strongly now than a feeble whisper, but shakily. 'I thought I was dying.'

'And you sent for me because you believed you'd been poisoned. Who, Miss Goff?'

'I went to see that woman. I couldn't do anything, go to the office, until I was satisfied she knew what the position was.'

'When you left me?'

'Yes.'

'About the house?'

'Yes. She took me by surprise rather . . . as though we were old friends. She asked me in and said that in our different ways we'd both been fond of Richard and that it was wrong if we now fought over his poor dead body. She offered me a drink and when I said I didn't, insisted on getting coffee and biscuits for us both. I was a fool, but I didn't for one minute think . . .' She grimaced. 'After the coffee she even offered me one of those cheroot things she smokes.'

'And you took it?' There went the evidence of a mysterious cigar-smoking visitor and he should have discovered that earlier.

'Yes. I wanted to be as friendly as I was able.'

With one whom she had called a scheming whore, he thought, as far from understanding women as ever. 'The coffee, Miss Goff. You didn't taste anything?'

'No, it seemed perfectly normal.' She groaned softly and bit at her lip. 'God! I feel rotten.'

'I'm sorry. How did she serve it? From a percolator?'

'In cups. She left me and presumably poured it in the kitchen

. . . brought them in on a tray.'

'And what was the conversation about while you drank it?'

'She was telling me how she'd reported Richard missing, how anxious she had been and how shocked when you'd told her he had been killed and buried in someone else's grave. She said she understood how I must feel about everything that had happened in the past but she had never influenced Richard in any way, that it was he who had insisted on her changing her name.' Her voice sounded incredulous. 'You know, I was beginning to believe her, thinking that I had misjudged her. That is, until I told her that, naturally, I was proposing to move back into the house and expected her to go.' She licked her mouth. 'Could you give me a drink, please?'

He poured water into a glass from a jug on the locker and held it to her lips, watching impatiently as she sipped it slowly.

'What did she say to that?' he asked, replacing the glass she had emptied.

'She told me that it was quite out of the question, that she had been paying rent to Richard for the rooms and facilities she used for her experiments and had documents to prove it, that she proposed remaining there as a paying tenant. When I told her that Richard had intended selling the house she said she knew that, but it had been unlikely he could with her having a legal right to part of it. Can she do that?' she asked.

'That's civil law,' he said, 'and I don't know. But I'm afraid it sounds a bit of a toss-up between the two of you because you did leave the house voluntarily.'

'I was forced to, Mr Rogers. She also said that she had a right to claim on Richard's estate, having cohabited with him for six years and paid for things to be done to the house.' Her eyes were pleading with him to tell her that this was nonsense.

'I don't know about that either, but anything is likely when lawyers get their teeth into it.' He disliked handing out false assurances and couldn't lie to her. He thought that it would be difficult to dislodge Mrs Knostig legally. 'I presume that things then became a bit heated?'

'Yes.' She showed a flash of venom. 'I told her that the house was now mine and that I'd have her ejected. She was furious, said all manner of vile things to me, screamed at me and said . . . she said she'd see me dead first.' Her fingers plucked at the bedclothes. 'She nearly did, didn't she?'

'Was Miss Blandford in the house?'

'I imagine she was. I heard somebody moving around in another room when I arrived.'

'She would have known you were with Mrs Tillman?'

'I'm sure she would. I drove up to the front of the house and knocked on the door. And I heard talking when that woman went out to make the coffee.' Her eyelids were drooping. 'I'm tired,' she said, 'and not feeling well.'

'I won't be much longer,' he promised. He felt as she said she did, but at least with an expectation of a bacon-and-egg breakfast, strong hot coffee and a first-of-the-day pipe of tobacco to banish it. 'What did you do when you left?'

'I drove home – it was late and I had to be in my office at ten. I got ready and left.'

'Did you eat or drink anything before leaving?'

'I didn't have time.'

'You felt all right?'

'Perfectly.'

'And you collapsed at your office?'

'Yes,' she said and for a moment her eyes relived it. 'It came on suddenly. I felt really dreadful . . . sick in my stomach and dizzy. I thought of what you said . . . how Richard was killed.'

'What time was that?'

She made an involuntary move to look at the watch no longer on her wrist. 'About one o'clock I think. I'm not quite sure.'

'That would be five hours or so after you'd drunk the coffee?'

She was clearly not capable of working that out. 'Yes . . . I suppose so.'

'And when you got here you told the doctor you'd been poisoned?'

157

'Yes, he didn't appear to know what was wrong with me.'

Fair enough, Rogers agreed mentally. It could have been anything. But not fair enough that he had neglected to preserve it when he'd got it out of her.

'I was *frightened*, Mr Rogers,' she whispered. 'So awfully frightened. What a dreadful thing to do to anyone. I *am* going to get better, aren't I?'

'Yes,' he said, 'I'm sure you are. What did Mrs Tillman . . .'

The door opened and Sister Anderson came in bustling. His time was up and there were to be no concessions. He stood, sure that he was creaking audibly. He hadn't got all that he wanted, but enough to be able to do something about a supposedly intelligent woman so surprisingly capable of blatant stupidity in her wickedness.

27

Before taking a hurried breakfast of sausage, kidney and eggs in the Mess – a working breakfast, Rogers called it, because he was thinking out his case while he ate – he had sent for Lingard.

He had used the telephone, at the same time mowing one-handed his stubble with his office shaver, to dispatch a Detective Sergeant and a D./P.C. chosen for their burliness and determination to bring Wimbush in for questioning before he left his tool-shed bed. He expected to have a charge to prefer against him and any resistance to his invitation to come quietly would, he hoped, prove fairly painful.

Lingard found his senior finishing his final cup of coffee and dabbing his mouth with a force-crested napkin. 'You've eaten, David?' Rogers asked, rising from the table. In theory, a good officer always looked after the welfare of his men, and horses when they had them, before himself.

'If I had, you'd have had me shot.' Lingard was the antithesis of the neglected Rogers, managing to look well scrubbed, closely shaved and immaculate.

'Yes, I would. Unfortunately there's no time for you to eat now. I'm being pushed into action without enough ammunition.' He scowled his disapproval of being committed to premature confrontation. 'I'll tell you about it on the way.'

The gates of Nympton Manor were open and Rogers drove through them along the weed-grown drive. Lingard, at his side, was replenishing his nostrils with Attar of Roses for the third time in lieu of his missed breakfast.

Rogers glanced across the lawn as they passed for scarred turf or broken bushes outside the tool shed. Seeing none, he accepted that Wimbush had gone without a struggle.

Pulling to a halt at the steps, he said, 'No relaxed sphincter, David. This woman's a cannibal with policemen.' Close to, the house showed its dilapidated and paint-blistered decrepitude in the morning's sun which promised a sweltering day, the leaves of the creeper around the windows already starting to droop.

As he climbed from the car, so the door with the tarnished knocker opened and Mrs Knostig stood there, her face dark with anger. She was wearing her blue shirt and woollen skirt, beginning now to look as though she slept in them. Before he reached her, with Lingard following behind, she snapped, 'I've been trying to get you on the telephone. What have you done with my gardener?'

'Good morning, Mrs Knostig,' he said. She would always be that in his thinking. 'I imagine you saw it?'

'Too late to stop it. They were your men, of course.' She was working herself into a fury, blotches of pink over her cheekbones. 'How *dare* you do that!'

'I might explain,' he said equably, 'if you'll not shout at me. I

159

want to speak to you about Mr Knostig's death. Not,' he added, 'on the doorstep.' He held her stare, beating down any objection she might have.

She tightened her lips and turned and he followed her in with Lingard closing the door behind them. If the living-room had been tidied since his last visit it showed no signs of it, its disorder being exposed brightly in the sunshine pouring through the open windows. Glittering motes of dust floated in its bars as they moved on the carpet.

She stood foursquare and formidable in the middle of the room, facing the two men. There was no invitation to sit, the line of her antagonism towards them already clearly drawn. Rogers thought he had been wrong in attributing rhinoceros-like qualities to her; she was definitely all piranha fish.

'I said I wanted to speak to you about Mr Knostig's death,' he said, now having to choose his words with caution. 'We now believe that he died of poisoning.'

The anger in her expression changed to disbelief. 'Poison!' she repeated. 'You believe? Don't you know?'

'I've also reason to believe that when you reported missing the man you call your husband, you knew that he was already dead and buried in Saint Boniface's churchyard. That he died in his bedroom here from the effects of that poison.'

Her chin lifted and she glared at him. 'No!' she said violently. 'How dare you say that! How dare you!'

How dare he indeed. He believed it, was convinced of it, but could prove none of it. She was, as he had anticipated, going to be obdurate in her denials and, in his experience, obduracy in a woman was never moved by opposing facts. Which he didn't have anyway. He was already believing that there was much merit in the use of the rack and thumbscrews.

'Further,' he continued, ignoring her outburst, 'that you and one other person removed him from this house during the night of Thursday last, took his body to the churchyard and buried it.'

'I refuse to listen to your ridiculous allegations.' Her voice

160

was shaking with her anger, her fingers moving at her sides in a jerky rhythm.

'You may do so, but I shall make them.' He spoke with an unemotional civility, outwardly impassive but, inside, praying fervently that he was not making a mind-boggling balls-up of it. Lingard, standing near the window, was inhaling his snuff and Rogers wished that he himself were the uncommitted observer and not the one who could be wrong, on whom the law's doom and disaster would descend for any unsupported accusations of a crime against a woman later proved to be of spotless character. In a more conversational tone of voice, he said, 'If you report that a husband has gone missing, would you agree it would be necessary to suggest that he had enough ready money on him to be in a position to do it? Particularly if it was later found that he hadn't cashed a cheque or used his Cashpoint card.'

There was a tightening of her face, nothing more.

'A dead husband, even a common-law one, with an existing wife would give you immediate problems with solicitors over the ownership of the house, with the Inland Revenue, with his bank. Missing and not found, you can stretch it to seven years before he could be legally presumed dead. Are you with me, Mrs Knostig?'

'I said I would not listen to your ridiculous allegations,' she said harshly.

'So you did,' he conceded mildly. 'And wouldn't his death be more advantageous to your occupancy here than his selling the house?'

Her mouth twitched, then compressed and she shook her head.

'You are, I imagine, familiar with the plant known as bittersweet? You have access to it?'

'Of course.' She was still aggressive, not wilting with guilty knowledge. 'I use it as one of my food-plants.'

'And know it to be poisonous to human beings?'

'Are you telling me that is what he was poisoned with?'

He couldn't, but he had seen a brief creasing of her forehead. 'He was in his pyjamas when he died. Is that why you refused me permission to look in his bedroom?'

'I refused you because I could see no reason why you should. That is still the case and you still cannot.'

'Your husband's Citroën was checked being driven towards the railway station at 2.40 a.m. on Friday. It was being followed by another car.'

'Are you suggesting I was driving it?' She made it a resolute riposte and he suspected she was searching for how much he really knew.

'Yes, I am,' he said firmly. 'Were you?'

'No, I was not.'

'Or the second car?'

She gave him a basilisk glare meant to discompose him.

He was beginning to sweat beneath his shirt, not certain that it was solely from the sun. A hectoring interrogation – which was not his method anyway – would be as unlikely to get an admission from this tough-fibred woman as were his formal questions. That she had side-stepped a couple of them might indicate areas of sensitivity. Or might not. Detectives, he thought, should be blessed with one of the attributes of God, able to read what truths lurked in a sinner's mind.

'Why do you call yourself Mrs Knostig and not Mrs Tillman?' he asked.

'Because I choose to.' She made it sound like 'Mind your own bloody business.'

'And for much the same reason Mrs Knostig proper calls herself Miss Goff?'

She said nothing to that.

'Miss Goff was here last night.'

'Was she?' The woman was giving him nothing.

'She is now in hospital and is alleging that you put poison in her coffee.'

There was a complete cessation of movement in her until she stiffened, her hands clenching into fists and her face flinching as if struck. A dull flush of red appeared on her throat where an artery pulsed her perturbation. 'No,' she choked. 'I did not.' Her mouth tightened against its shaking and she looked around her as though seeking escape from him.

For a moment, Rogers felt pity for her as he would for any woman fighting against cataclysmic trouble. There was no point in going on with his futile questioning. It was mind-making-up time and he was about to jump a fence without knowing what was on the other side. It would be a holding charge of dubious authority until he sorted things out and he wasn't happy about it.

'I'm arresting you, Mrs Knostig,' he said, 'on suspicion of being concerned in the death and unlawful burial of Richard Knostig. I have to tell you that you are not obliged . . .'

His recital was interrupted by the slamming of a car's door and the repeated coughing sound of an engine being started from the back of the house. 'David!' he snapped, 'quick!' and Lingard was through the door, his footfalls receding rapidly along the hall. Simultaneously, he heard the low gear racing, echoing in a confined space and its acceleration fading away to silence.

'That was Miss Blandford,' he said. 'Has she taken your car?' He should have had her collected when he arrived, but panic flight had never been written in his picture of her. She had probably been listening outside the door again.

Mrs Knostig stared at him stonily, but with a shadow of unease in her eyes.

He made a noise of self-disgust in his throat. 'As you wish,' he said. 'I have to tell you that you are not obliged to say anything unless you wish to do so, but what you say may be put into writing and given in evidence. You understand?'

She nodded, appearing to have pulled herself together, her fears – if she had any – repressed and looking as bloody-mindedly intractable as she had for most of the interview. 'I have nothing to say,' she said in a strong voice, 'until I have spoken to my solicitor.'

Lingard re-entered the room, caught Rogers's eye and gave a single shake of his head. 'Too late,' he said. 'I didn't even see it. Miss Blandford?'

'Yes, and it doesn't matter. I can guess where to. You telephone for transport and a policewoman and take Mrs Knostig into custody.' He spoke to the woman. 'In the meantime, I propose looking at your husband's bedroom and in the kitchen.'

'You will not,' she exploded angrily. 'I refuse to allow you, you contemptible bully!'

'The house belongs to the legal Mrs Knostig and I'm quite certain she would have no objection,' he said unruffled. 'I have also a right to search for articles under the control of an arrested person.'

Turning and leaving her, he heard her saying hard words at Lingard as he walked quickly along the hall.

He found the kitchen at the rear of the house, its window overlooking a walled yard and a garage with its doors wide open. From which, it was obvious, Helen Blandford had driven the car. The kitchen was neglected to the same degree of slovenliness as every room other than the laboratory; the cooking utensils, the food mixer, liquidizers and deep fryer indifferently cleaned and left around without order or method. Nothing was revolting filthy, but Rogers concluded that housekeeping was patently being ignored by intellects more occupied with the weighty matter of cutting up moths. The cutlery, plates and beakers of an uncleared breakfast lay on the table. The huge pantry was an uninvestigable chaos of jars, cans and packets of food, food wrapped and unwrapped together with a few pellets of the droppings of mice who were surviving whatever warfare was being waged against them. No receptacle containing anything that could be recognized as a liquid poison was in the kitchen and he had not expected to find it.

Having satisfied himself with the contents of one particular cupboard, he returned to the hall and climbed the stairs. The long landing, empty of anything but the carpeting and a few pictures, had five doors in it. The first he opened was a bathroom smelling of scented soap, the bath still moist with blobs of foam in its base.

Peering around the second door, he saw a double bed – guessing it to be the marital bed from which Knostig had been ejected – and a dressing-table with a woman's sprays and cosmetic containers on it. Two pillows showed side by side under the bed cover but that, he assured himself, did not necessarily confirm Humfries' suspicion that the two women slept together. The room had in it a lingering smell of a woman's body and nothing of the scent worn by Helen Blandford.

The third door he opened revealed a single bed, a small table at its side on which stood a reading lamp, a few paperbacks and a glass ashtray, a wardrobe and a chest of drawers. It wasn't a room of sybaritic luxury or one in which Rogers could imagine furtive extra-marital carnality.

He entered it and opened the wardrobe, confirming Knostig's former occupancy of the room by the row of men's jackets and trousers in it. On the floor, concealed in a recess, were Irish whiskey bottles; two unopened, the others empty. Not, Rogers considered, the most original of hiding places for a man living with a woman who objected to his drinking the stuff, and she must have known had she bothered to look.

The bed sheets and pillow slip were freshly laundered and uncreased by a sleeping body. He removed the slip and examined the pillow inside, finding nothing on it. There were no pyjamas in the bed, though he found three pairs in a drawer. There were no spectacles or case for them on the table and nowhere else that he had looked with the missing wallet in mind.

He crouched and stared intently at the carpeting at the side of the bed, smoothing it with the flat of his hand. After doing the same with the blue rug on the opposite side, he lifted it and examined the carpeting beneath. With his head pressed to it, he could see obliquely a faint darker stain the size of a saucer in the expanse of green fibres. It could be vestigial vomit, scrubbed to remove it and now dry. Only the laboratory physicist, were he available, would be able to tell him for certain.

Getting to his feet, grunting at the ligaments aching in his knee joints, he replaced the rug over the stain. Without giving him the feeling that he had wrapped things up to a satisfactory conclusion, he was a milligram or so happier about having chanced his arm and arrested Mrs Knostig.

28

She had told Rogers that when she wished to get away from people she went to Kirk's Pipe on the moor. It was a likelier place to look than any other of which he knew nothing. Although it seemed excessive, the thought of her being there now had in it an ominous background of desperation heading for a suicidal leap into its dark depths. As the fear gained conviction he pushed his car above the limit in the outskirts of the town, abusing himself for wasting time in his search for the evidence of Knostig's dying.

With the last of the houses behind him he pressed hard on the accelerator, fighting to keep out of his mind the picture of her broken and bleeding body lying in the bottom of the pipe with the mouldering bones of dead sheep. After the longest and slowest eleven miles he hoped not to have to do again, he turned off the road on to the track that led steeply to where he hoped she might not be. Despite the open window at his side and his jacket removed to lie on the passenger seat, he sweated.

As he climbed the track became steeper and narrower, degenerating into something he considered should be restricted to goats. The car's suspension creaked and banged, the wheels throwing up stones to rattle against the underbody and, it being his own car, he suffered that too. With the ground dropping away behind him, his view was a panoramic one of rising green and purple moorland, of a brazen sun in a vast expanse of blue sky. The warm perfume of grasses and heather came in through the window. It was not the milieu for the recall of murderous malice and a decaying dead body in a mortuary, of moonlit graveyards and secret burials. Nor, he thought unhappily, of squalid copulation in a tool shed.

The metallic gold Capri parked on the track, hot air still rippling from its bonnet, was not one he had seen before, but he had no doubts. He halted close behind it and, dismounting from his car, removed the key left in the Capri's ignition. Looking up the steep slope he saw her, a small white-dressed figure sitting on an outcrop of limestone. She must have seen him approach but remained motionless and, he thought, watching him.

Because there were ugly sweat stains in the armpits of his shirt and he felt a need for official formality, he put on his jacket. He climbed the slope towards her, brushing through the grass and heather that clung to his trouser-legs, the sharp stones hurting his feet through shoes meant only for walking on carpets and cement footpaths. His lungs, accustomed to the town's carbon monoxide and his tobacco smoke, were working hard in coping with the gradient. He was high enough now to see far below the town as a huge sprawling spider of slate and brick baking in the sun, blotched with green only where tame trees were allowed to grow.

Nearing her, he knew he had worried unnecessarily about her jumping into the pipe. She was sitting relaxed with her back to it. Had she wished to, she need only lean backwards far enough to drop into its depths, and had she intended to, she would surely have done so on his approach.

Willing to carry his official manner only so far, he sat at her side on the warm stone. Not too close, he made certain, to the small-girl body with its disturbing sensuality too inadequately covered by the white dress. Her arms and legs were bare and she had kicked off her shoes. The non-duty part of his mind noted that her feet were the uniform brown of her legs.

'You know?' she asked calmly.

'Yes,' he said, hoping that he did. 'Why did you do it?'

'For Olivia, naturally.' She said it as though it explained everything. 'I'd do anything for her. What did you do to her?'

'She's been arrested.'

'Poor Olivia. I thought she would be. And now you've come to arrest me?'

'Isn't that why you took off in her car?'

'Partly. How did you know I was here?'

'You mentioned it once and I thought . . .' He glanced involuntarily into the dark hole. 'I thought you'd be here to, well, to think about things.'

She turned her head and looked down it too. 'You thought I . . . down *there*?'

He shrugged, damning her feminine perception. 'You can never be certain with people in trouble.'

'But you wanted to save me.' A slight edge of mockery was in her voice. She wasn't anything like uncovered culpability fleeing the scene and was either harder than he had thought her or more stupid.

'I came here to arrest you. And to ask you questions.'

'The mole digging for worms again?' That hadn't apparently worried her either. 'I'm quite prepared to tell you everything. It was so difficult before, having to protect Olivia.'

'And yourself.' He remembered how subtly she had steered him towards her discarded boyfriend Humfries in doing it.

'You shouldn't be surprised at that.'

'I'm not. So are you going to tell me about it?'

'Will you help me?'

'No bargains and no haggling,' he said. 'You please yourself. In fact, I'm telling you now that you aren't obliged to say anything unless you wish to do so, but whatever you do say may be given in evidence.' The required cautioning was, he knew, as effective a way of telling a suspect to shut up as anything he knew. It could throw a large spanner in the workings of justice.

168

Now it sounded archaic and stilted in the hot sunshine and clean air.

'I see.' She was thoughtful. 'But you'd still arrest me whether I do or not?'

'Who knows? You might convince me against the facts.' Facts, he thought. He couldn't remember finding one he could use. 'You have the opportunity now of explaining how and why. From the beginning,' he added.

'I heard you tell Olivia that Richard had been poisoned,' she said, 'but I still can't understand it. I didn't have anything to do with that. You do believe me, don't you?'

'Never ask a policeman that. We aren't programmed for it, only to suspend our belief.'

'But you don't think so?'

'Miss Blandford,' he said patiently, 'you mustn't cross-examine me about my opinions. I'm not supposed to have any. I'm a collector of facts and truths, nothing more.' She was being as difficult as Mrs Knostig, if in a more pleasant way.

'I only wanted to know.' She said it in a rebuffed small-girl voice.

'Start, if you wish, from when he returned home.'

'I don't know when he did. I went to bed early that night – about ten o'clock I think.'

'With Olivia still downstairs?' He had never imagined calling the formidable woman that, but it made for a distinction between the two Mrs Knostigs.

'I left her reading in the sitting-room.'

'And you didn't hear him come in?'

'No.'

'So when did you know he'd returned?'

'I didn't actually know until . . . that is, he never came down to breakfast and Olivia didn't mention him until we were in the laboratory. Then she began to get irritable because she wanted him to mist spray the pupae in the cages. I remember she said damn him and his hangovers, or something like that. After a while she went upstairs to wake him up. She came down after a

169

few minutes in a terrible state. She couldn't tell me for some time. Then she said, "Oh, my God! Richard's dead. He's up there on the floor." She was white and trembling and I fetched her a whisky. I'm sure it was a terrible shock to her.'

'And to you?' The sun was hot on his back and he could see small globules of perspiration glistening like butter on her skin in the V of her dress.

'Naturally, yes. But being concerned about Olivia, it didn't affect me so much. When she calmed down she said, "What are we going to do, Helen? Where can we go?" She meant with our research. It's her life. All she has, really, and she has to have a laboratory to qualify for the university grant.'

'She was thinking about his legal wife claiming the house?'

'Yes. With Richard dead it would be difficult to stay there. Not impossible, but difficult. And she has very little money, you know.'

'But he had intended selling the house. Wouldn't that have made it even more inevitable? That must have occurred to her. To you both.'

'Yes,' she said reluctantly, 'I suppose it did.'

'What did you do about Richard dead on the floor?'

'I went upstairs with her. I'd never seen anybody dead before.' Her face twitched with remembered revulsion.

'He was in his pyjamas?'

'Yes. There was sick on them and his face . . .' Her throat worked and she turned her head away from him. 'I asked Olivia how he'd died and she said because he'd been drunk again and had suffocated . . . regurgitated his vomit, she said.'

'You didn't question that?'

'How could I? It's possible, I suppose. I couldn't think that she had done it. I don't now.'

'Would you have helped her had you?'

'I don't think so. No, I wouldn't.' She sounded sincere and her eyes held frankness, but Rogers knew that could mean nothing.

170

'You were looking at the body,' he reminded her, 'and wondering what to do.'

'Yes. Olivia said, "I'm not going to let it happen. We've got to hide him." We went back downstairs and talked about it and the more we talked the more necessary it seemed to be.'

'For her or the two of you?' So far she had admitted nothing factually but a knowledge of Knostig's death, although she had not resisted his statement that she had helped Mrs Knostig.

'I was quite prepared to help her. Olivia's my dearest friend and I'd do very very much for her.'

'Such as helping to bury Richard?' He made that a proven fact known to him.

She hesitated, indecision in her expression. 'I didn't think of that as being particularly wrong Olivia said that legally the Church of England hadn't a monopoly on burying people.'

'They haven't, of course, but a do-it-yourself burial happens to be unlawful. Tell me how you decided where to bury him.'

'Olivia knew that Wimbush's uncle – I think he was his uncle – had been buried the week before . . .'

'Because she'd given him the afternoon off to attend it?'

'Yes. She thought that nobody would find Richard there.' She shuddered and licked her lips. 'You're making me go through it all over again. I don't know how I did it, but I helped her take off his pyjamas and dress him. And to wash his face. That was dreadful.' She reached and grasped his arm momentarily. 'Having to touch him, to see his face. We drank lots of whisky. It was the only way. And it was so difficult – even burning his pyjamas.'

There was silence between them and, as he thought, he looked down the steep slope to where the two cars glittered in the sun. Nose to tail on the track they could suggest, he realized, two metallic animals in an unintended and unforeseen attitude of intimacy. He envied the fat bees pollen-collecting in the flowers of the heather at his feet. They had no problems, only simple untroubled motivations; no female with limpid brown eyes and a disturbing body to unsettle a man's mind, to make difficult the gathering of his particular pollen.

'You forgot his spectacles,' he said, breaking the silence.

'Yes. Olivia found them afterwards and took them away with her.'

'Because I'd asked about them?'

'Yes.'

'And his wallet?'

'She took that with his other stuff. There were only a few pounds in it and it seemed a waste to bury it with him.'

'And it would have identified him had he been found in a few years' time.' He could smell her scent, see peripherally her eyes on him and knew that she would use them emotionally to cozen him. With an aloof impassivity he stared at the view in front of him. 'Go on with getting rid of him,' he said.

'Olivia and I went to the churchyard in the evening while it was still light to see where the new grave was and how we could do it.'

'In her car.' Rogers knew that he had slipped a little there. It hadn't occurred to him that a daylight reconnaissance might be considered necessary. They or the easily-remembered gold Capri could well have been seen by the Reverend Gathercole vigilantly watchful over his dead flock.

'Yes,' she said. 'When it was late enough we carried him downstairs and outside and laid him in the back of his car.' Her eyes shadowed and she ground her jaw muscles. 'Olivia drove it and I followed in the Capri. I thought we'd be stopped by the police for something, but we weren't. There was nobody about and she drove through the gate to the church door. We lifted him out and put him in the porch, then drove the cars into the road behind so that nobody would see them near the church.'

'What about the spades?'

'We only had one and a plastic sheet. I left it in the porch with Richard. When we came back we saw a man standing at the gate. It was moonlight and we could see he wasn't a policeman.

A weird man in a cloak and a funny hat. He was trying to open the gate and was having difficulty with it. We stood and watched him go in out of our sight, petrified with Richard being in the porch. There was nothing we could do but wait. It was frightening and I thought I was going to be sick. I wanted to run away, but Olivia was wonderful. She was frightened too, but said we should wait, we had no choice.' She paused, then said, 'Have you a cigarette? I came out without mine.'

He gave her the packet of ten he carried with him for these occasions (although a defending barrister had once accused him of inducing a confession with them) and, when she had taken one, held a match to it. He avoided her eyes searching his over the small flame. Men fell easily into a woman's eyes so close, so demanding with whatever message they carried. He needed a smoke himself but kept his pipe in his pocket.

'The man in the churchyard,' he prompted her. Poor old Lockersbie wouldn't appreciate being called weird.

'We knew,' she continued, 'that if he saw Richard's body he would go running for the police. When he came out a very short time afterwards he was acting as if he was drunk. He didn't look as though he'd seen Richard, but leaned against the wall for a long time. I thought he'd never go. When he did he just wandered off and Olivia said she was sure that he hadn't seen Richard, that he'd gone in there to spend a penny. We hurried then and carried Richard to the grave. He was appallingly heavy because we were getting tired, but somehow that wasn't the worst part. We couldn't be seen behind the trees and we pulled the grass covering off, then shovelled the earth on the plastic sheet. We didn't need a light, only when Olivia tidied up later while I kept watch at the gate in case the police came. A car did come along and we panicked dreadfully, but it went by.' She shivered. 'I don't know how we did it. Olivia said a prayer over him. She cared that much, even if you don't think so.'

He didn't think so. Prayers said over the body of the man the two women both disliked sounded mawkish to him. 'Then you took the Citroën to the station car park?'

'Olivia did, and I followed in her car to bring her back to the house. She thought it would look as though Richard had gone off somewhere by train. When we got back we drank half a bottle of whisky between us, cried a little, had a bath and went to bed.'

He had a mental picture of them drunkenly lustful in the bath together – he had seen only one bathroom – and cursed his prurient mind. Surely not; not having just returned from burying a dead man. And also not because he knew that the chemistry of his body would never respond to that of a lesbian's. He sat silent and unconsciously frowning, trying to fit what she had told him into the framework of what he knew. A curlew's melancholy cry, heard clearly in the distance, emphasized the emptiness of the moor. It seemed to isolate him from the town below and all its requirements and obligations. He thought more of the woman at his side. He needed to convince himself that this appetite he felt for her was solely his satyriasis breaking the bounds of its discipline, that in different circumstances, as a man and not a buttoned-up copper, a couple of furious nights in her bed would burn it out of his system without leaving ash.

She broke in on his thoughts. 'I'm not sorry, you know,' she said. 'We weren't hurting Richard.'

'No, but you were concealing the commission of a serious crime.'

'I didn't know that.'

'And proposing to steal from his wife what was legally hers.'

'I didn't see it like that.'

He studied her face and she stared back at him gravely. 'It's not me you'll have to convince,' he said. 'Did you know his wife?'

'I'd never met her. He hadn't lived with her for years.'

'Were you in the house last night when she called?'

'I was in the laboratory writing up my notes. I heard the car arrive and her knocking at the door. I thought it was you at first.'

'You saw her?'

'No. Olivia came in and said she was there. I assumed she didn't wish me to see her.'

'No more?'

'No. Just that. I was going to see . . . I was going out anyway.'

'Did she take anything from the laboratory?'

She looked puzzled. 'Like what?'

'Like anything at all.'

'No, definitely not. I remember she looked around the door, not actually coming in.'

'Did she make you a coffee?'

'Why should she? We'd already had it.'

So leave it at that, for he wasn't prepared to browbeat her. There had been something defensive in her voice. She must have heard him questioning Mrs Knostig about it and had gone out immediately afterwards. Hearing all that he had said could explain her unusually forthcoming admission about Knostig's burial. The slab on which they sat was hard and his buttocks felt numbed. He grimaced as though that were the reason and shifted his position, leaving a wider gap between them.

'You said you were going out,' he said woodenly. 'Was that to see Wimbush in the tool shed?'

There was a long pause before she spoke, visibly shaken, her bottom lip unsteady. 'It was you! Damn you! How could you?'

'I'm sorry. I didn't know you were in there.'

She looked at him, her eyes seeking something in his. 'It wasn't what you are thinking. Is that why he was arrested?'

'He was arrested on the strength of my *not* thinking it. Why?'

'I did telephone you last night,' she said. 'When I heard your voice, I . . . I couldn't tell you. He spoke to me during the afternoon and said that he'd been in the shed that night, that he'd seen Olivia and me leaving in the cars and also coming back. He said that he was worried about whether it was his duty to tell the police, that so far he had been telling lies for me. He was so abominably slimy. He said I must go to the shed when it was dark to talk about what he should do. I knew what he meant . . . it was in his vile face. That's why I telephoned you, intending to tell you the truth. But then I thought of Olivia and the trouble she would be in, losing her laboratory for sure, going to prison, if it all came out.' She shrugged sadly. 'I don't mean to sound terribly noble, because I'm not. Although it was a disgusting thing to have to do, if it was going to keep him quiet it was worth it. And for my part as well. I'm only sorry that you know about it,' she said forlornly. 'I hate him, the filthy pig. And it was all for nothing.'

He believed her, recognizing that he did so because he wanted to. But believing also that at some time her body must have responded to the masculinity of even a slimy Wimbush and that would always be a black worm in his mind. 'When this is over,' he said, 'I shall want you to give that in evidence. It was a criminal offence and he's to be punished.' But it would not, he knew, be punishment as mercilessly physical as he himself would like to inflict.

'I don't care what happens to him.' Her eyes were soft on his, an intent in them to collide emotionally with him. 'You don't understand. It's your knowing that matters.'

'No.' She was going to say things he didn't wish to hear and he made his voice sharp. 'It doesn't matter. It never has.'

'It does to me. You must know why . . .'

It was she who didn't understand that he was required to be an emasculated policeman who got his pleasures from arresting villains and putting them in cells. That even if he were not, the memory of that moonlit vignette of squalid carnality would always inhibit him with her.

He stood and held her arm briefly in a symbolic gesture of arrest, lifting her to her feet. 'We have to go,' he said gently. 'Don't be sad. It'll all come out right in the end.' And that was a

reassuring banality with nothing much of the truth behind it.
Rogers knew that life was rarely so obliging with people in
trouble.

29

Having completed his preliminary paperwork, Rogers remained at his desk, staring into the empty bowl of his pipe. He
called it thinking things out.

Continuing to believe that Knostig had been murdered by
the use of a vegetable poison – please God that Bridget knew her
stuff – he was still without proof that he definitely had. Given
that he had been buried secretly to circumvent the disposal of
Nympton Manor – and he had only Helen Blandford's admission on that – he could no longer presume confidently that he
had been murdered. Even with death by poisoning proved
eventually by the laboratory scientists, it could be argued that
an unloved and desperate Knostig had, with his marital and
financial problems, the pressures of a pregnant mistress,
enough darkness in his soul to commit suicide. It had been done
for much less.

His investigation had reached an impasse. There was a limit
to how far he could go on acting on suspicion only and he had
already pushed it to the edge of the reasonable. Theory,
whether feather-light or solidly logical, carried no weight as an
excuse for being wrong and, he reminded himself, nobody's
future was so overlookable as that of an unsuccessful detective's.

That he had four bodies in the cells on holding charges –
Humfries for stealing cheques, Wimbush for procuring a
woman by threats to have sexual intercourse with him, and
Olivia Knostig and Helen Blandford for conspiring to prevent

the lawful burial of a corpse – gave him no great comfort. Exaggerating wryly, he reflected that Detective Superintendent George Rogers was now in open country, vulnerable to being sprayed with shot by a Police Complaints Board, the Ecclesiastical Commissioners, the National Council of Civil Liberties, whatever trades unions actors and jobbing gardeners belonged to and, possibly, whoever it was who caused belittling injuries to a male's ego under the Sex Discrimination Act.

Not a man to dive into the shrubbery for cover until actually being shot at, he put on his jacket and left the office for his car.

30

She was sitting on the chair at the side of the bed when Rogers entered the small ward. With a washed-out pink bathrobe over her nightdress, her hair had been fashioned back into its bouffant tidiness, her mauve lipstick restored and she wore her spectacles.

Unsmiling, he said, 'Good afternoon, Miss Goff,' and stood with his back to the open window where the hospital smells lost most of their unpleasantness. 'I understand from the doctor that you are being discharged.'

Her plump face was less pale than it had been earlier, any expression withheld from it in reacting to his unannounced presence, for he must appear to her an unwelcome black bird of ill omen.

'Yes,' she said, 'but I'm still feeling unwell.'

No matter how much she might have recovered, the interrogation of a woman in hospital – an emotive phrase in the mouth of a lawyer, suggesting helpless femininity being badgered by a brutal constabulary – would be seized upon as a harassment and that he wasn't proposing to risk. But he had to know, to satisfy himself, before she was discharged and returned to her home.

He spoke with deliberation. 'Nothing of what I say or what you say will be admissible in evidence, Miss Goff, but I have to put certain facts and conclusions to you. You may answer or not as you choose.' Why, he thought, did official formality make him sound so bloody pompous?

'I don't know what you mean,' she said, but her expression said that she did.

He moved sideways from the window, leaving her in the full flood of sunshine, her features in its revealing light. 'Mrs Tillman is in custody. She has not been charged either with the murder of your husband or with attempting to murder you. Nor will she be, despite your allegation against her this morning, your attempt to involve her in crimes she did not commit.' He had stuck his neck out with a vengeance and he waited for her angry denials.

There were none. Her lips had tightened and she said, 'I see,' with nothing of agreement or disagreement in her words.

'I'll tell you why, Miss Goff. Much of it will be by implication with which you may disagree. You'll be given the opportunity later to do so.' He now had to be careful not to disclose the paucity of his facts. 'The rights and wrongs of your leaving your husband are immaterial, but you did leave him in possession of the house with Mrs Tillman in residence as his mistress. Understandable, I suppose, but ill-advised. So long as your husband lived and she remained his mistress she had a sort of security for herself and her research. With your husband dead she would have none of it, for you as his legal wife would have first claim on his property. And this assumes that he made no will. Or, if he did, that you were the beneficiary anyway.' He cocked his head for an answer.

'He made no will,' she said flatly. 'He never would.'

'From Mrs Tillman's point of view,' he continued, 'his death must have been calamitous, the writing on the wall. He came back to the house on the Wednesday night, went to his bedroom – he slept alone, incidentally – and died during the night. That, being discovered by Mrs Tillman the following morning, might have meant the end of her occupation of Nympton Manor and, apparently, the withdrawal of the grant subsidizing her research.'

He couldn't put into a policeman's words for this woman the despair Mrs Tillman must have felt, possibly her irrational anger at Knostig's being so inconsiderate as to die. He could understand and go part of the way with her thinking in what she had eventually decided.

'What she didn't know was that he had been poisoned. By you, the previous evening.'

No protest, no denial; only the folding of her arms over her breasts as though to protect them. The window, reflected in her spectacle lenses, made her eyes unreadable. She had almost certainly anticipated the probability of being questioned and had determined her attitude beforehand.

'I believe that the non-events of the following day and the day after that pushed you into telephoning Nympton Manor to find out what had happened. The silence must have been disconcerting for you. Somebody should have told you something by then and you didn't know whether he had died or not. If he hadn't, he would probably know or guess that it had been you who had poisoned him. When Mrs Tillman told you that he was dead and that we were investigating it, that must have frightened you.' Even somebody as cold-blooded as you, he said in his mind. 'So you rang again to find out why. And that was when you were told he'd been missing from home and had been found dead. That had to put you in a quandary, for you didn't know where and how. And being known by Mrs Tillman to know that your husband was dead under suspicious circumstances, you had no option but to come and see me. When I told you . . .'

An air liner was climbing on its take-off from the airport, its thundering jets blotting out his words and vibrating the window-frame at his side. He waited until it had passed, not taking his eyes from the motionless woman in the chair for whom the noise seemed not to exist.

'When I told you that he'd been poisoned and secretly buried,' he continued as though there had been no interruption, 'you guessed by whom. And that played right into your hands. Mrs Tillman had buried him, therefore it would be logical to anyone that she had also poisoned him. Even Miss Blandford suspected that she had.' He waited a few moments for taut silence to work on her thinking. 'What *did* you poison him with?' he pushed at her sternly. 'An extract of deadly night-shade? Bittersweet? You'd know all about those, wouldn't you? You'd worked long enough with food-plants for butterflies and moths before Mrs Tillman took over.'

'You told me I need not answer.' She appeared completely insensitive to his accusations and, apart from the absence of any sign of outraged innocence, he could believe that he had got it all wrong. She was the type of woman he had dealt with seldom, although often enough to accept that behind the soft plumpness there could be impenetrable obduracy – he equated it with mulish stupidity – against which mere persuasion would ricochet. Trying to enter her mind was like forcing open a padlocked ice-box. And he had only her word for it that she didn't like killing butterflies and shedding green blood.

'So I did,' he said, 'and that still goes. But you could say that I'm here as a prodder to your conscience. No? All right, I'll go on. Your husband visited you that night and he'd told you he was coming. I don't believe it was to discuss his anxiety to have you back with him. Everything I know is against it. He wanted a divorce – possibly on the grounds of your deserting him – and no doubt told you why. Did he?' He was thinking of the pregnant Charlotte Inglis and Knostig's imperative need to do something about her.

Her unblinking stare was a kind of answer for, he knew, she could have denied it without committing herself to anything.

'That would have been fatal to your chance of getting the

house back, wouldn't it? And there was also his intent to sell it. That too was a threat to you. I can't think of anything more certain than that your husband's death would be all to your advantage and to nobody's else's.'

She gave him a single angry shake of her head and he held back a sigh. Who was it he was thinking about? Sisyphus or some other silly bugger who spent his life pushing rocks up a steep hill, only to have them roll down again. Whoever he had been, he should have been called Rogers.

'I imagine that you gave him the stuff in coffee,' he went on. 'He began to show signs of it an hour or so after he left you.' Although it had obviously been she to whom the soon-to-be-dead Knostig had referred as a 'bloody obstinate bitch', he decided not to toss her that as well. 'You would know, of course, that you don't drop stone dead in your tracks with vegetable poisoning, that it needs time to take effect. Which is very helpful when whoever it is doesn't live with you and is going somewhere else to die. But all your efforts seemed to be going for nothing when you called on Mrs Tillman last night. It wasn't a social call and it was against the warning I gave you. On your own admission she'd infuriated you when she told you she wasn't getting out of the house you considered yours, that she had a claim on your husband's estate and intended pursuing it. I imagine you'd have poisoned *her* given the opportunity. Instead, when you returned home you took a weak dose of it to implicate her further. Dangerous, Miss Goff? Not very when you know what you're doing. It'll give you the symptoms and you can exaggerate those. Not very dangerous either when you're certain of immediate medical attention and make sure that it's known you've been given poison. It was a gamble, but worth the risk. Particularly so when it would divert any possible suspicion from your having used it on your husband.' He frowned at her. 'And expecting that having told me what you did, that at some time you'd be giving evidence on oath against an innocent woman.'

He paused. The ward sister, not so attractive or friendly as

Morag who had gone off duty, had stopped at the door and was peering through the glass panel. Obviously, he told himself, to ensure that he wasn't jumping on a helpless patient's face. The patient, a withdrawn island of plump flesh in the waiting silence, either didn't know or couldn't care. Rogers stared the sister out of countenance and she left.

'Not much more,' he said. 'Mrs Tillman and Miss Blandford had already eaten and had had their after-dinner coffee when you called. Even disregarding that, and that there could have been no anticipating your visit, it's highly unlikely that Mrs Tillman would offer you coffee or anything but her dislike. Which we agree is a two-way thing and you certainly didn't go there for a cosy chat. I don't make too much of it, but you made an understandable mistake in lying about it. A small one and it doesn't help you. Mrs Tillman possesses no coffee cups. I know because I've looked. Only rather peculiar beakers difficult to accept as cups. You've no comment on that either?'

It was less rewarding than having a conversation with a brick wall, and a brick wall wouldn't make him feel so much the heavy-handed inquisitor of a virtually defenceless woman. She was obviously not to be moved by the logic of his unmasking of her wickedness and if she remained silent he could foresee serious difficulties in proving a case against her.

She surprised him by saying in a firm voice, 'I do have a comment. Are you going to arrest me?'

'Not at the moment. When I consider it necessary.'

'I'm not a fool, superintendent,' she said contemptuously. 'That means you have no evidence. Nor could there be.'

He moved to the door and stood holding the handle. He had one bullet left and it could miss by yards, but he fired it. 'I'm sure,' he said, 'that nobody can brew up a poison in their home without leaving traces of it for a laboratory chemist to identify. A warrant to search your flat is already being sworn out this afternoon and a policewoman is waiting in the corridor to escort you there. I shall be . . .'

He cut his words short as he saw her face change, her

obduracy shattered startlingly like fragile glass at her realization of what she had overlooked. A silent cry of anguish formed in her opened mouth, the confirmed truth of what he was saying in her shocked eyes and in the pinching of her nostrils.

'It's there, isn't it?' he asked, the unnecessary question of the day.

She moaned, rocking her body back and forth violently. Then she looked up at him, her spectacles askew, a strand of her hair fallen loose. 'I had to do it,' she wailed. 'Don't you understand? I didn't want to, but I *had* to.'

She seemed to shrivel in her chair even as he regarded her with the beginnings of a pity for what she would now have to suffer. Self-justification was going to be some sort of a comfort to her and it wasn't in him to destroy it. He could afford not to, for it had been her dead husband who had been the loser, not him. 'I understand,' he said agreeably, 'Of course I do.'

31

Lingard had been called out to the scene of the reported suicide of a man who had been found in the canal, head downwards and tied by one wrist to a 12-volt car battery. Unless Lingard had doubts, Rogers decided that he might justifiably skip that one for the paperwork he had to do.

His desk was dusty and untidy with uncollected cups, an unemptied ashtray and an overflowing IN tray. As with the staff of the Forensic Science Laboratory, the Headquarters' civilian cleaners and clerical workers were absent for the weekend. It never failed to irritate him. On the desk, sealed and labelled in a plastic bag and going some way to mollifying him, was a small aluminium saucepan with the residue of a pale-yellow liquid in it. He had found it, looking like urine and smelling weakly of boiled leaves, on the bottom shelf of Miss Goff's larder. She had not denied that it was the remains of the potion she had put into coffee for her husband and of which she herself had drunk a teaspoonful.

She had been stupid in her villainy, but not so much so that her goose was irretrievably cooked. She had refused to make a written statement, so it might never be cooked. Rogers had few doubts that any counsel instructed for her defence could convince a jury that she had given her husband what the counsel would miscall a simple herbal infusion in the mistaken belief that it was either an aphrodisiac or a cure for his excessive drinking. And if that looked like failing, there was always the bolt-hole of diminished responsibility.

Olivia Knostig and Helen Blandford had been recharged with disposing of a corpse with intent to prevent a coroner's inquest and Rogers had then delegated to the Duty Chief Inspector their release on bail, not seeing either of them again. Theirs had been a relatively minor offence and he had convinced himself that he had also to have some consideration for the welfare of the moths and caterpillars left to fend for themselves in an empty house. He would now never know – and didn't wish to know – whether Helen Blandford had liked him as a man or had been seeking to cozen him as a policeman. A delicate *amour propre* required a certain amount of protection.

There was an administrative problem he needed to resolve. Brooker, the detective who had been instructed to check the grave in which Knostig had subsequently been found, had not only neglected his duty, he had lied about it. And either offence deserved a disciplinary charge and his transfer from the Department. He had told Rogers that he had visited the grave hourly from 10 p.m. until his discovery of the exposed hand at 3 a.m. That had been the lie, and it was one which Rogers could not openly refute.

Recalling it now in prosaic daylight, he could still shudder.

At 1.15 at night with eerie moonlight casting black shadows in the lonely graveyard it had been different. Dressed in the darkest clothing he possessed, he had climbed over the wall and, discarding dignity, had crawled on hands and knees between the headstones and bushes to Harland's grave. There, he had dug with a trowel and his bare hands beneath the turf, feeling down ghoulishly in the loose soil for dead flesh. Christ! Even thinking about it at his desk brought back the fearful anticipation that he would actually find it, touch it; the sickening grubbing for the feel of a decaying body.

The smell of corruption had come first and that made the vomit rise in his throat. It could have come from the coffined Harland, and it had taken all his need to find Knostig without further delay to keep him there. It had been cold sweat, a thumping heart and the back of his neck prickling his horror; even irrational fears of his hands being grasped from below in the earth, of being dragged down into the grave.

When his searching fingers touched cloth with solidness beneath it he had nearly yelled his revulsion. But better than having found the dead face, which he had feared. Forcing himself to work along what he recognized to be an arm, he had reached a cold hand. A helping hand, he had called it sardonically even in his nausea, dragging it out into the moonlight and staring hypnotically at its pathetic horribleness for long moments before he could decide that it might with persuasion appear to have been dug up by a hungry fox. And then finding the time to be 1.50 and Brooker almost due, racing back to get to his house for the telephone call that hadn't come until after three o'clock. By which time he had drunk three strong whiskies, undressed for bed and fallen asleep in the waiting.

That had recurred in the nightmarish dream of last night and would, he was sure, recur again tonight. There was only one prophylactic he knew for nightmares. It would be available were Lingard not to decide that the man in the canal hadn't gone in voluntarily and if coaxing words could persuade Bridget to call at his home late that night to discuss again the pathological aspects of Knostig's death over a couple of drinks. He reached for the telephone and dialled her number with more hope than optimism.